S0-BCT-300

DOUBLE DEUCE

OTHER BOOKS BY ROBERT B. PARKER

Pastime
Perchance to Dream (a Philip Marlowe novel)
Stardust
Poodle Springs (with Raymond Chandler)
Playmates
Crimson Joy
Pale Kings and Princes
Taming a Sea-Horse
A Catskill Eagle
Valediction
Love and Glory
The Widening Gyre
Ceremony
A Savage Place
Early Autumn
Looking for Rachel Wallace
Wilderness
The Judas Goat
Three Weeks in Spring (with Joan Parker)
Promised Land
Mortal Stakes
God Save the Child
The Godwulf Manuscript

Robert B. Parker

DOUBLE
DEUCE

G. P. PUTNAM'S SONS
New York

G. P. Putnam's Sons
Publishers Since 1838
200 Madison Avenue
New York, NY 10016

Copyright © 1992 by Robert B. Parker
All rights reserved. This book, or parts thereof,
may not be reproduced in any form without permission.
Published simultaneously in Canada

Library of Congress Cataloging-in-Publication Data

Parker, Robert B., date.
Double deuce/ Robert B. Parker
p.   cm.
ISBN 0-399-13721-1.—ISBN 0-399-13754-8 (limited ed.)
I. Title.
PS3566.A686D6   1992   91-29594 CIP
813′ .54—dc20

Printed in the United States of America
1   2   3   4   5   6   7   8   9   10

This book is printed on acid-free paper.
∞

For Karen Panasevich, who taught me
about youth gangs, and about commitment.
And for my wife and sons, who have taught
me everything else that matters.

DOUBLE DEUCE

PROLOGUE

Her name was Devona Jefferson. She was going to be fifteen years old on April 23, and she had a daughter, three months and ten days old, whom she had named Crystal, after a white woman on television. Crystal had the same dark chocolate skin her mother had, and the large eyes. She probably looked like her father too, because some of her didn't look like Devona. But Devona didn't know which one the father was, and she didn't care, because Crystal was all hers anyway, the first thing she'd ever had that was all hers.

She loved carrying Crystal, loved the weight of her, the smell of her hair, the soft spot still in the back of her skull, where the white lady doctor at City had told her the skull hadn't grown together yet. They were together most of the time, because there was no one to leave Crystal with, but Devona didn't mind much. Crystal was a quiet baby, and Devona would carry her around and talk with her, about their life together and what it would be like when Crystal got bigger and how they'd be friends when Crystal grew up, because they'd be only fourteen years apart.

She had Crystal dressed that day in a new snowsuit with a little hood that she'd bought at Filene's with money she'd gotten from a boyfriend named Tallboy who dealt dope and might be Crystal's father. It was white satin with lace at the hood, and she liked the way Crystal's face looked, so black in the middle of the white satin. Devona had on a pink sweatsuit with pink high-cut sneakers that she wore with rainbow shoelaces. It was a warm spring and she wasn't wearing anything over the sweatsuit, even though she had Crystal bundled in her snowsuit.

She was on Hobart Street. It wasn't her turf, but she wasn't down special with one gang, and she might have even duked one of the Hobart Street Fros sometime. She wasn't sure. Still she felt the little tight feeling in her stomach when the van crawled up behind her and followed along as she walked. She always felt a little protected when she had Crystal. People were usually more careful about a baby, and she always felt like she could protect her baby, which made her feel like she could protect herself.

She rounded the corner by Double Deuce with the spring sun warm in her face. The van came around behind her. Somebody spoke to her from the passenger side.

"You Tallboy's slut?"

"I not no one's slut," she said. "I Crystal's momma."

Somebody else in the van said, "Yeah, she's Tallboy's." And something exploded in her head.

She never heard the shots that killed her, and killed Crystal. There were twelve of them, fired as fast as the trigger would pull, from a 9mm semiautomatic pistol through the back side door of the van. Devona fell on top of her baby, but it didn't matter. Three slugs penetrated her body and lodged in the baby's chest, one of them in her heart. Their blood was mixed on the sidewalk outside Twenty-two Hobart Street, when the first cruiser arrived. It wasn't until the wagon came and they moved her to put her on the litter that anyone even knew the baby was there and they had two homicides and not one.

CHAPTER

1

Hawk and I were running along the river in April. It was early, before the Spandex-Walkman group was awake. The sunshine was a little thin where it reflected off the water, but it had promise, and the plantings along the Esplanade were beginning to revive.

"Winter's first green is gold," I said to Hawk.

"Sure," he said.

He ran as he did everything, as if he'd been born to do it, designed for the task by a clever and symmetrical god. He was breathing easily, and running effortlessly. The only sign of energy expended was the sweat that brightened his face and shaved head.

"You working on anything?" Hawk said.

"I was thinking about breakfast," I said.

"I might need some support," Hawk said.

"You might?"

"Yeah. Pay's lousy."

"How much?" I said.

"I'm getting nothing."

"I'll take half," I said.

"You ain't worth half," Hawk said. "Besides I got the job and already put in a lot of time on it. Give you a third."

"Cheap bastard," I said.

"Take it or leave it," Hawk said.

"Okay," I said, "you got me over a barrel. I'm in for a third."

Hawk smiled and with his arm at his side turned his hand palm up backhand. I slapped it lightly once.

"Housing project called Double Deuce," Hawk said. "You know it?"

"Twenty-two Hobart Street," I said.

We were running past the lagoon now, on the outer peninsula. There were ducks there, pleased with the spring, paddling vigorously, and regularly sticking their heads underwater, just for the hell of it.

"Ever been in Double Deuce?"

"No."

Hawk nodded and smiled. "Nobody goes in there. Cops don't go in there, even black cops, except in pairs. Only people go in there are the ones that live there, which is mostly women and small children. And the gangs."

16

"The gangs run it," I said.

"For a little while longer," Hawk said.

"Then who's going to run it?"

"We is."

We went over the footbridge from the lagoon and rejoined the main body of the Esplanade. There were several sea gulls up on the grass, trying to pass for ducks, and failing. It didn't matter there was nobody feeding either of them at this hour.

"You and me?" I said.

"Un huh."

"Which will require us, first, to clean out the gangs."

"Un huh."

"We got any help on this?"

"Sure," Hawk said. "I got you, and you got me."

"Perfect," I said. "Why are we doing this?"

"Fourteen-year-old kid got killed, and her baby, drive-by shooting."

"Gang?" I said.

"Probably. Church group in the neighborhood, women mostly, some kind of minister, couple of deacons. They got together, decided to stand up to the gangs. Neighborhood watch, public vigil, shit like that."

"Bet that brought the Homeboys to their knees," I said.

"There was another drive-by and one of the deacons got kneecapped."

"Which probably cut back on the turnout for the next vigil," I said.

"Sharply," Hawk said. "And they talk to the Housing

17

Police and the Boston Police and . . ." Hawk shrugged. "So the minister he ask around and he come up with my name, and we talk, and he hire me at the aforementioned sum, which I'm generously sharing with you 'cause I know you need the work."

"What do they want done?"

"They want the murderer of the kid and her baby brought to, ah, justice. And they want the gangs out of the project."

"You got a plan?" I said.

"Figure you and me go talk with the minister and the church folks, and then we work one out."

The traffic was just starting to accumulate on Storrow Drive and the first of the young female joggers had appeared. Colorful tights stretched smoothly over tight backsides.

"The gangs don't scare us?" I said.

"I a brother," Hawk said.

"Double Deuce doesn't scare you?" I said.

"No more than you," Hawk said.

"Uh oh!" I said.

2

Susan and I were sitting on her back steps, throwing the ball for Pearl, Susan's German Short Hair. This was more complicated than it had to be because Pearl had the part about chasing the ball and picking it up; but she did not have the part about bringing it back and giving it to you. She wanted you to chase her and pry it loose from her jaws. Which was not restful.

"She can be taught," Susan said.

"You think anyone can be taught," I said. "And you think you can do it."

"You have occasionally shaken my confidence," Susan said. "But generally that's true."

She had on nearly knee-high black boots and some sort of designer jeans that fit like nylons, and a windbreaker that looked like denim and was made of silk, which puzzled me. I'd have thought it should be the other way around. Her thick black hair had recently been cut, and was now a relatively short mass of curls around her face. Her eyes remained huge and bottomless. She had a cup of hot water with lemon which she held in both hands and sipped occasionally. I was drinking coffee.

"Got any thoughts on gangs?" I said.

"Gangs?"

"Yeah, youth gangs," I said.

"Very little," Susan said.

Pearl came close and then shied away when Susan reached for the ball.

"You're a shrink," I said. "You're supposed to know about human behavior."

"I can't even figure out this dog," Susan said. "Why do you want to know about gangs?"

"Hawk and I are going to rid a housing project of them."

"How nice," Susan said. "Maybe it could become a subspecialty for you. In addition to leaping tall buildings at a single bound."

"Spenser's the name. Gangs are the game," I said. "You know anything about youth gangs?"

"No," Susan said. "I don't think many people do. There's a lot of literature. Mostly sociology, but my business is essentially with individuals."

"Mine too," I said.

Pearl came to me with the yellow tennis ball chomped in one side of her mouth, and pushed her nose under my forearm, which caused my coffee to slop from the cup onto my thigh. I put the cup down and reached for the ball and she turned her head away.

"Isn't that adorable," Susan said.

I feinted with my right and grabbed at the ball with my left, Pearl moved her head a quarter inch and I missed again.

"I haven't been this outclassed since I fought Joe Walcott," I said.

Susan got up and went into her kitchen and came out with a damp towel and rubbed out the coffee stain in my jeans.

"That was kind of exciting," I said.

"You want to tell me about this gang thing you're involved in?"

"Sure," I said. "If you'll keep rubbing the coffee stain out of my thigh while I do it."

She didn't but I told her anyway.

While I told her Pearl went across the yard and dropped the tennis ball and looked at it and barked at it. A robin settled on the fence near her and she spotted it and went into her point, foot raised, head and tail extended, like a hunting print. Susan nudged me and nodded at her. I picked up a pebble and tossed it at the robin and said "Bang" as it flew up. Pearl looked after it and then back at me.

"Do you really think the 'bang' fooled her?" Susan said.

"If I fired a real gun she'd run like hell," I said.

"Oh, yes," Susan said.

We were quiet. In the *Globe* I had read that coffee wasn't bad for you after all. I was celebrating by drinking some, in the middle of the morning. Susan had made it for me: instant coffee in the microwave with condensed skim milk instead of cream. But it was still coffee and it was still officially not bad for me.

"I don't see how you and Hawk are going to do that," Susan said.

"I don't either, yet."

"I mean the police gang units in major cities can't prevent gangs. How do you two think you can?"

"Well, for one thing it is we two," I said.

"I'll concede that," Susan said.

"Secondly, the cops are coping with many gangs in a whole city. We only have to worry about the gangs' impact on Double Deuce."

"But even if you succeed, and I don't see how you can, won't it just drive them into another neighborhood? Where they will terrorize other people?"

"That's the kind of problem the cops have," I said. "They are supposed to protect all the people. That's not Hawk's problem or mine. We only have to protect the people in Double Deuce."

"But other people deserve it just as much."

"If the best interest of a patient," I said, "conflicts with the best interest of a nonpatient, what do you do?"

Susan smiled. "I am guided always," she said, "by the

22

best interest of my patient. It is the only way I can do my work."

I nodded.

Pearl picked up the tennis ball and went to the corner of the yard near the still barren grape arbor and dug a hole and buried the ball.

"Do you suppose that this is her final statement on chase-the-bally?" I said.

"I think she's just given up trying to train us," Susan said. "And is putting it in storage until someone smarter shows up."

"Which should be soon," I said.

3

Twenty-two Hobart Street is a collection, actually, of six-story brick rectangles, grouped around an asphalt courtyard. Only one of the buildings fronted Hobart Street. The rest fronted the courtyard. Therefore the whole complex had come to be known as Twenty-two Hobart, or Double Deuce. A lot of the windowglass had been replaced by plywood. The urban planners who had built it to rescue the poor from the consequences of their indolence had fashioned it of materials calculated to endure the known propensity of the poor to ungraciously damage the abodes so generously provided them. Everything was brick and cement and cinderblock and asphalt and metal. Except the windows. The place had all the warmth of a cyanide factory. To the bewilderment of the urban planners, the poor didn't like it there much, and after they'd broken most of the windows, everyone who could get out, got out.

Hawk parked his Jag at the curb under a streetlight and we got out.

"Walk in here," Hawk said, "and you could be anywhere. Any city."

"Except some are higher."

"Except for that," Hawk said.

There was absolutely no life in the courtyard. It was lit by the one security spotlight that no one had been able to break yet. It was littered with beer cans and Seven-up bottles and empty jugs of Mogen David wine. There were sandwich wrappers and the incorruptible plastic hamburger cartons that would be here long after the last ding dong of eternity.

The meeting was in what the urban planners had originally no doubt called the rec room, and, in fact, the vestige of a Ping-Pong table was tipped up against the cinderblock wall at the rear of the room. The walls were painted dark green to discourage graffiti, so the graffiti artists had simply opted for Day-Glo spray paints in contrasting colors. The Celotex ceiling had been pulled down, and most of the metal grid on which the ceiling tiles had rested was bent and twisted. In places long sections of it hung down hazardously. There were recessed light cans with no bulbs in amongst the jumble of broken gridwork. The room light came from a couple of clamp-on portable lights at the end of extension cords. In the middle of the room, in an incomplete circle, a dozen unmatched chairs, mostly straight-backed kitchen chairs, had been set up. All but two of the chairs were occupied. All the occupants were black. I was with Hawk. He was black. I was not. And rarely had I noticed it so forcefully.

A fat black man stood as Hawk and I came in. His head was shaved like Hawk's and he had a full beard. He wore a dark three-piece suit and a pastel flowered tie. His white-on-white shirt had a wide spread collar, and gold cuff links with diamond chips glinted at his wrists. When he spoke he sounded like Paul Robeson, which pleased him.

"Come," he said. "Sit here."

I already knew who he was. He was the Reverend Orestes Tillis. He knew who I was and didn't seem to like it.

"You Spenser?"

"Yes."

"This is our community action committee," Tillis said to Hawk. He didn't look at me again.

An old man, third from the left, wearing a Celtics warm-up jacket that had ridden up over the bulge of his stomach, said, "What's the face doing here?"

I looked at Hawk.

"That you," he said and smiled his wide happy smile.

"When Hawk mentioned him," Tillis said, "I assumed him to be a brother."

"You the man?" the old guy said.

"No," I said.

"Don't see why we need some high-priced face down here telling us how to live."

"He's with me," Hawk said.

"Too many goddamn fancy pants uptown faces come down here in their goddamn three-piece suits telling us how to live," the old man said. I was wearing jeans and a leather jacket. The rest of the committee made a sort of neutralized supportive sound.

"Gee," I said. "They don't like me either."

"I can't take you anywhere," Hawk said. He turned toward the old guy and said quietly, "He with me."

The old guy said, "So what?"

Hawk gazed at him quietly for a moment and the old guy shifted in his seat and then, slowly, began nodding his head.

"Sure," he said. "Sure enough."

Hawk said, "I come over here to bail your asses out, and Spenser come with me, because I hired him to, and we probably the only two people in America can bail your asses out. So you tell us your situation, and who giving you grief, and then you sort of get back out the way, and we get to bailing."

"I want to be on record, 'fore we start," Tillis said. "I got no truck with the white Satan. I don't want no help from him, and I don't trust no brother who get help from him. White men can't help us solve our troubles. They the source of our troubles."

"Price you paying," Hawk said. "Can't afford to be too choosy."

27

"I don't like the face," Tillis said.

I was leaning on the wall with my arms folded.

Hawk gazed pleasantly at Tillis for a moment.

"Orestes," he said. "Shut the fuck up."

There was a soft intake of breath in the room. Hawk and Tillis locked eyes for a moment. Then Tillis turned away.

"I'm on the record," he said, and went and sat on a chair in the front row.

"Now," Hawk said, "anybody got an idea who killed this little girl and her baby?"

"Cops know?" I said.

A woman said, "You know, everybody know."

She had long graceful legs and a thick body, and her skin was the color of coffee ice cream.

"It's the Hobarts, or the Silks, or some other bunch of gangbangers that keep changing the name of the gangs so fast I can't keep track. And how we supposed to stand up to them? We a bunch of women and old men and little kids. How we supposed to make some kind of life here when the gangbangers fuck with us whenever they feel like?"

"They don't fuck with me," the old man said.

"Course they do," the woman said. "You old and fat and you can't do nothing about it. That's why you here. They ain't no men here, 'cept a few old fat ones that couldn't run off."

The old man looked at the ground and didn't say anything, but he shook his head stubbornly.

"They got guns," another woman said. She was smallish and wore tight red pants that came to the middle of her calves and she had two small children in her lap. Both children wore only diapers. They sat quietly, squirming a little, but mostly just sitting staring with surprising dullness at nothing very much. "They got machine guns and rifles and I don't know what kinds of guns they all are."

"And they run the project," Hawk said.

"They run everything," the big woman said. "They own the corridors, the stairwells. They'd own the elevators, if the elevators worked, which a course they don't."

"They got parents?" I said.

Nobody looked at me. The woman with the thick body answered the question, but she answered it to Hawk.

"Ain't no difference they got *parents*," she repeated my word with scorn. "Some do. Some don't. Parents can't do nothing about it, if they do got 'em. How come you brought him here? Reverend didn't tell us we'd have to talk to no white people. White people don't know nothing."

"He knows enough," Hawk said. "Name some names."

The group was silent. One of the babies coughed and his mother patted him on the back. The big-bodied woman with the graceful legs shifted in her seat a little bit. The old guy glowered at the floor. Everyone else sat staring hard at nothing.

"That get a little dangerous, naming names?" Hawk said. He looked at the Reverend Tillis.

Tillis was standing with his hands behind his back, gazing solemnly at the group. He shook his head sadly, as if he would have liked to speak up but grave responsibilities prevented him.

"Sure," Hawk said. "Anybody got an idea why the kid and her baby got shot?"

Nobody said anything.

Hawk looked at me. I shrugged.

"Me and Satan gonna be around here most of the time the next few weeks," Hawk said. "Till we get things straightened out. You have any thoughts be sure to tell us. Either one of us. You talk to Spenser, be like talking to me."

Nobody said anything. Everyone stared at us blankly, except Tillis, who looked at me and didn't like what he saw.

4

We came out of the meeting at about 9:30. It was a fine spring night in the ghetto. And around Hawk's car ten young men in black LA Raider caps were enjoying it.

A big young guy, an obvious body builder, with a scar along his jawline and his hat on backwards, was sitting on the trunk of the car.

As we approached he said, "This you ride, man?"

Hawk took his car keys out of his pocket with his left hand. Without breaking stride he punched the kid full in the face with his right hand. The kid tipped over backwards and fell off the trunk. Hawk put the key in the lock, popped the trunk, and took out a matte finish Smith and Wesson pump-action 12 gauge shotgun. With the car keys still dangling from the little finger of his left hand, he jacked a round up into the chamber.

The kid he had punched was on his hands and knees. He shook his head slowly back and forth, trying to get the chimes to stop. The rest of the gang was frozen in place under the muzzle of the shotgun.

"You Hobarts?" Hawk said.

Nobody spoke. I stood half facing Hawk so I could see behind us. I didn't have my gun out, but my jacket was open. Hawk took a step forward and jammed the muzzle of the shotgun up under the soft tissue area of the chin of a tall kid with close-cropped hair and very black skin.

"You a Hobart?" Hawk said.

The kid tried to nod but the pressure of the gun prevented it. So he said, "Yeah."

"Fine," Hawk said and removed the gun barrel. He held the shotgun easily in front of him with one hand while he put his car keys in his pocket. Then without moving his eyes from the gang he reached over with his left hand and gently closed the trunk lid.

"Name's Hawk," he said. He jerked his head at me. "His name's Spenser."

The kid who'd taken the punch had gotten to his feet and edged to the fringe of the group where he stood, shaky and unfocused, shielded by his friends.

"There some rules you probably didn't know about, 'cause nobody told you. So we come to tell you."

Hawk paused and let his eyes pass along the assembled

gang. He looked at each one carefully, making eye contact.

"Satan," he said, "you care to, ah, promulgate the first rule?"

"As I understand it," I said. I was still watching behind us. "The first rule is, don't sit on Hawk's car."

Hawk smiled widely. "Just so," he said. Again the slow scan of tight black faces. "Any questions?"

"Yeah."

The speaker was the size of a tall welterweight. Which gave Hawk and me maybe sixty pounds on him. He had thick hair and light skin. He wore his Raiders cap bill forward, the old-fashioned way. He had on Adidas high cuts, and stone-washed jeans, and a satin Chicago Bulls warm-up jacket. He had very sharp features and a long face and he looked to be maybe twenty.

Hawk said, "What's your name?"

"Major."

"What's your question, Major?" Hawk showed no sign that the shotgun might be heavy to hold with one hand.

"You a white man's nigger?" Major said.

If the question annoyed Hawk he didn't show it. Which meant nothing. He never showed anything, anyway.

"I suppose you could say I'm nobody's nigger," Hawk said. "How about you?"

"How come you brought him with you?" Major said.

"Company," Hawk said. "You run this outfit?"

I knew he did. So did Hawk. There was something in the way he held himself. And he wasn't scared. Not being

33

scared of Hawk is a rare commodity and is generally a bad mistake. But the kid was real. He wasn't scared.

"We all together here, man. You got some problem with that?"

Hawk shook his head. He smiled. Uncle Hawk. In a minute he'd be telling them Br'er Rabbit stories.

"Not yet," he said.

Major grinned back at Hawk.

"Not sure John Porter believe that entirely," he said and jerked his head at the guy that had been sitting on Hawk's trunk.

"He's not dead," Hawk said.

Major nodded.

"Okay, he be bruising your ride, now he ain't. What you want here?"

"We the new Department of Public Safety," Hawk said.

"Which means what?"

"Which means that starting right now, you obey the 11th commandment or we bust your ass."

"You Iron?" Major said.

"We the Iron here," Hawk said.

"What's the 11th commandment?"

"Leave everybody else the fuck alone," Hawk said.

"You and Irish?" Major said.

"Un huh."

"Two guys?"

"Un huh."

Major laughed and turned to the kid next to him and put out his hand for a low five, which he got, and returned vigorously.

"Good luck to you, motherfuckers," he said, and laughed again and jerked his head at the other kids. They dispersed into the project, and the sound of their laughter trailed back out of the darkness.

"Scared hell out of him, didn't we?" I said.

"Call it a draw," Hawk said.

5

"She was hit seven times," Belson said. He was sitting at his desk in the homicide squad room, looking at the detectives' report from the Devona Jefferson homicide. "They fired more than that. We found ten shell casings, and the crime-scene techs found a slug in the Double Deuce courtyard. Casings were Remington—nine-millimeter Luger, center-fires, 115-grain metal case."

"Browning?" I said.

Belson shrugged.

"Most nines fire the same load," he said. "Whoever shot her probably emptied the piece. Most nines carry thirteen

to eighteen in the magazine, and some of the casings probably ejected into the vehicle. Some of the slugs went where
we couldn't find them. Happens all the time."

Belson was clean-shaven, but at midday there was already a five o'clock shadow darkening his thin face. He was
chewing on a small ugly cold cigar.

"Baby took three, through the mother's body. They were
both dead before they hit the ground."

"Suspects?" I said.

I was drinking coffee from a Styrofoam cup. Belson had
some in the same kind of cup, because I'd brought some for
both of us from the Dunkin Donut shop on Boylston Street
near the Public Library. I had cream and sugar. Belson
drank his black.

"Probably she was shot from a van that drove by slowly
with the back door open."

"Gang?"

"Probably."

"Hobarts?"

"Probably."

"Got any evidence?"

"None."

"Any theories?"

"Gang people figure it's a punishment shooting," Belson
said. "Maybe she had a boyfriend that did something
wrong. Probably drug related. Almost always is."

"They got any suspects?"

"Specific ones? No."

"But they think it's the Hobarts."

"Yeah," Belson said. "Double Deuce is their turf. Anything goes down there it's usually them."

"Investigation ongoing?" I said.

"Sure," Belson said. "City unleashes everything on a shine killing in the ghetto. Treat it just like a couple of white kids got killed in the Back Bay. Pull out all the stops."

"Homicide got anybody on it?" I said.

"Full time?" Belson smiled without meaning it, and shook his head. "District boys are keeping the file open, though."

"Good to know," I said.

"Yeah," Belson said. "Now that you're on it, I imagine they'll relax."

"I hope so," I said. "I wouldn't want one of them to start an actual investigation and confuse everything."

Belson grinned.

"You come across anything, Quirk and I would be pleased to hear about it," he said.

"You're on the A list," I said.

6

I was in a cubicle at the Department of Youth Services, talking to a DYS caseworker named Arlene Rodriguez. She was a thin woman with a large chest and straight black hair pulled back tight into a braid in back. Her cheekbones were high and her eyes were black. She wore bright red lipstick. Her blouse was black. Her slacks were gray and tight and tucked into black boots. She wore no jewelry except a wide gold wedding band.

"Major is his real name," she said. She had a big manila folder open on her desk. "It sounds like a street handle but it's not. His given name is Major Johnson. In his first eighteen years he was arrested thirty-eight times. In the twenty-seven months preceding his eighteenth birthday he was arrested twenty times."

"When he turned eighteen he went off the list?" I said.

"He's no longer a juvenile," she said. "After that you'll have to see his probation officer or the youth gang unit at BPD."

"What were the offenses?" I said.

"All thirty-eight of them?"

"Just give me a sense of it," I said.

"Drugs, intent to sell . . . assault . . . assault . . . possession of burglary tools . . . possession of a machine gun . . . assault . . . suspicion of rape . . . suspicion armed robbery . . ." She shrugged. "You get the idea."

"How much time inside?" I said.

She glanced down at the folder on her desk.

"Six months," she said. "Juvenile Facility in Lakeville."

"Period?"

"Period," she said. "Probably the crimes were committed within the, ah, black community."

"Ah what a shame," I said. "Your work has made you cynical."

"Of course it has. Hasn't yours?"

"Certainly," I said. "You got any background on him— family, education, favorite food?"

"His mother's name was Celia Johnson. She bore him in August of 1971 when she was fifteen years and two months old. She was also addicted to PCP."

"Which meant he was, at birth," I said.

"Un huh. She dumped him with her mother, his grandmother, who was herself, at the time, thirty-two years old. Celia had three more babies before she was nineteen, all of them PCP addicted, all of them handed over to Grandma. One of them died by drowning. There was evidence of child abuse, including sodomy. Grandma was sent away for six months on a child-endangerment conviction."

"Six months?" I said.

"And three years' probation," Arlene Rodriguez said.

"Teach her," I said.

"His mother hanged herself about two months later, doesn't say why, though I seem to remember it had something to do with a boyfriend."

"So Major is on his own," I said.

Arlene Rodriguez looked down at her folder again.

"At eleven years and three months of age," she said.

"Anything else?"

"While we had him at Lakeville," she said, "we did some testing. He doesn't read very well, or he didn't then, but one of the testers devised ways to get around that, and around the cultural bias of the standard tests, and when she did, Major proved to be very smart. If IQ scores meant anything, which they don't, Major would have a very high IQ."

We were quiet. Around us there were other cubicles like this one, and other people like Arlene Rodriguez, whose business it was to deal with lives like Major Johnson's. The cubicle partitions were painted a garish assortment of bright reds and yellows and greens, in some bizarre bureaucratic conceit of cheeriness. The windows were

41

thick with grime, and the spring sunshine barely filtered through it to make pallid splashes on the gray metal desk tops.

"Any thoughts on how to deal with this kid?" I said.

Arlene Rodriguez shook her head.

"Any way to turn him around?" I said.

"No."

"Any way to save him?"

"No."

I sat for a moment, then I got up and shook her hand.

"Have a nice day," I said.

CHAPTER

7

Susan and I were walking Pearl along the Charles River on one of those retractable leashes which gave her the same illusion of freedom we all have, until she surged after a duck and came abruptly to the end of her tether. The evening had begun to gather, the commuter traffic on both sides of the river had reached the peak of its fever, and the low slant of setting sun made the river rosy.

I had the dog on my right arm, and Susan held my left hand.

"I've been thinking," she said.

"One should do that now and then," I said.

"I think it's time we moved in together."

I nodded at Pearl.

"For the sake of the child?" I said.

"Well, I know you're joking, but she's part of what has made me think about it. She's with me, she spends time with you. She's really our dog but she doesn't live with us."

"Sure she does," I said. "She lives with us serially."

"And we live with each other serially. Sometimes at my house, sometimes at yours, sometimes apart."

"The 'apart' is important too," I said.

"Because it makes the 'together' more intense?"

"Maybe," I said. This had the makings of a minefield. I was being very careful.

"Sort of a 'death is the mother of beauty' concept?"

"Might be," I said. We turned onto the Larz Anderson Bridge.

"That's an intellectual conceit and you know it," Susan said. "No one ever espoused that when death was at hand."

"Probably not," I said.

We were near the middle of the bridge. Pearl paused and stood on her hind legs and rested her forepaws on the low wall of the bridge and contemplated the river. I stopped to wait while she did this.

"Do we love each other?" Susan said.

"Yes."

"Are we monogamous?"

"Yes."

"Then why," Susan said, "aren't we domestic?"

"As in live together, share a bedroom, that kind of domestic?"

44

"Yes," Susan said. "Exactly that kind."

"I recall proposing such a possibility on Cape Cod fifteen years ago," I said.

"You proposed marriage," Susan said.

"Which involved living together," I said. "You declined."

"That was then," Susan said. "This is now."

Pearl dropped down from her contemplation of the river and moved on, snuffing after the possibility of a gum wrapper in the crevice between the sidewalk and the wall.

"Inarguable," I said.

"Besides, I'm not proposing marriage."

"This matters to you," I said.

"I have been alone since my divorce, almost twenty years. I would like to try what so many other people do routinely."

"We aren't the same people we were when I proposed marriage and you turned me down," I said.

"No. Things changed five years ago."

I nodded. We walked off the bridge and turned west along the south side of the river. We were closer to the outbound commuter traffic now, an unbroken stream of cars, pushing hard toward home, full of people who shared living space they shared.

"Trial period?" Susan said.

"And if it doesn't work, for whatever reason, either of us can call it off."

"And we return to living the way we do now," Susan said.

"Which ain't bad," I said.

45

"No, it's very good, but maybe this way will be better."

We swung down closer to the river so Pearl could scare a duck. Some joggers went by in the other direction. Pearl ignored them, concentrating on the duck.

"Will you move in with me?" Susan said.

We stopped while Pearl crept forward toward the duck. Susan kept hold of my left hand and moved herself in front of me and leaned against me and looked up at me, her eyes very large.

"Sure," I said.

"When?"

"Tomorrow," I said.

Pearl lunged suddenly against the leash, and the duck flew up and away. Pearl shook herself once, as if in celebration of a job well done. Susan leaned her head against my chest and put her arms around me. And we stood quietly for a moment until Pearl noticed and began to work her head in between us.

"Jealousy, thy name is canine," I said.

"Tomorrow?" Susan said.

"Tomorrow," I said.

Tomorrow . . . and tomorrow . . . and, after that, tomorrow. . . . Yikes!

8

Hawk and I sat in Hawk's car in the middle of the empty courtyard of Double Deuce. The only thing moving was an empty Styrofoam cup, tumbled weakly across the littered blacktop by the soft spring wind. The walls of the project were ornate with curlicued graffiti, the signature of the urban poor.

Kilroy was here.

There was almost no noise. Occasionally a child would wail.

"This is your plan?" I said to Hawk.

"You got a better idea?" Hawk said.

"No."

"Me either."

"So we sit here and await developments," I said.

"Un huh."

We sat. The wind shifted. The Styrofoam cup skittered slowly back across the blacktop.

"You got any thought on what developments we might be awaiting?" I said.

"No."

A rat appeared around the corner of one of the buildings and went swiftly to an overturned trash barrel. It plunged its upper body into the litter. Only its tail showed. The tail moved a little, back and forth, slowly. Then the rat backed out of the trash barrel and went away.

"Maybe we can keep the peace by sitting here in the middle of the project. And maybe we can find out who killed the two kids, mother and daughter," I said. "I doubt it, but maybe we can. Then what? We can't sit here twenty-four hours a day, seven days a week, until the social order changes. No matter how much fun we're having."

Hawk nodded. He was slouched in the driver's seat, his eyes half shut, at rest. He was perfectly capable of staying still for hours, and feeling rested, and missing nothing.

"Something will develop," Hawk said.

"Because we're here," I said.

"Un huh."

"They won't be able to tolerate us sitting here," I said.

Hawk grinned.

"We an affront to their dignity," he said.

"So they'll finally have to do something."

48

"Un huh."

"Which is what we're sitting here waiting for," I said.

"Un huh."

"Sort of like bait," I said.

"Exactly," Hawk said.

"What a dandy plan!"

"You got a better idea?" Hawk said.

"No."

"Me either."

9

When I got home Susan was in bed eating her supper and watching a movie on cable. Pearl was in bed with her watching closely. Susan was wearing one of my white shirts for a nightdress and her black hair had the sort of loose look it had when it had just been washed. I kissed her.

"And the baby," Susan said.

I kissed Pearl.

"There's some supper waiting for you in the refrigerator," she said.

"Good," I said.

"Why don't you get it and bring it up and we'll eat together and you can tell me about your day."

"I can tell you about my day now. Hawk and I sat for thirteen hours in the middle of Twenty-two Hobart Street."

"And?"

"And nothing. We just sat there."

"How boring," Susan said. "Well, get your supper and we can talk."

I took my gun off my belt and put it on the night-table next to my side of the bed. I took a shower. Then I went downstairs to the kitchen and found supper, a large bowl of cold pasta and chicken. I tasted it. There was raw broccoli in it, and raw carrots, and some sort of fat-free salad dressing that tasted like an analgesic balm. Susan admitted it tasted like an analgesic balm, but she said that with a little fat-free yogurt and some lemon juice and a dash of celery seed mixed in, it was good. I had never agreed with this. I put it back in the refrigerator. When I'd moved in I had brought with me a six-pack of Catamount Beer. I opened one.

In Susan's refrigerator was a half-used cellophane bag of shredded cabbage, some carrots, some broccoli, half a red pepper, half a yellow pepper, and half a green pepper, some skimmed milk, most of a loaf of seven-grain bread, and a package containing two boneless skinless chicken breasts. I sliced up both the chicken breasts on an angle, cut up the peppers, sprinkled everything with some fine herbs that I found in the back of Susan's cupboard, and put it in a fry pan on high. It was a pretty fry pan, a mauve color with a design on it, that went perfectly with the pillows on

51

the love seat in the kitchen. As an instrument for sautéeing it was nearly useless. I splashed a little beer in with the chicken and peppers and when it cooked away, I took the pan off the stove and made up a couple of sandwiches on the seven-grain bread. I put the sandwiches on a plate, got another beer, and took my supper upstairs.

"Oh, I left some pasta salad for you," Susan said.

"I sort of felt like a sandwich," I said.

Susan smiled and nodded. I sat on the edge of the bed and balanced the plate on the edge of the night-table. Pearl shifted on the bed and nosed at it. I told her not to and she withdrew nearly a quarter of an inch. I drank some beer and hunched over the plate, keeping my body between Pearl and the sandwich, and ate. It was not a neat sandwich and some of it fell on the night-table. I picked it up and gave it to Pearl.

The movie was some sort of love story between an elegant rich woman from Beverly Hills, who appeared to be 5'10", and a roughneck ironworker from Queens, who appeared to be 5'6". They were as convincing as Dan Quayle.

I finished my sandwich and got under the covers. Pearl got under the covers when I did, and stretched out between me and Susan.

"There appears to be a German Short Haired Pointer in bed with us," I said.

"That's where she sleeps," Susan said. "You know that."

I took the Globe from the floor beside the bed and opened it. The ironworker and the elegant lady were playing a love scene on the tube. I glanced at it. In the close-ups

52

he was much taller than she was. I went back to the paper. I noted in the TV listings that the Bulls were playing the Pistons on TNT.

"Why did you sit for all that time in the middle of the project?" Susan said.

"Hawk figures that it will make the gang react," I said.

"Isn't that sort of like being the bait in a trap?" Susan said.

"I raised that point," I said.

"And?"

"It is sort of like being bait," I said.

Susan was silent. Her eyes stayed on the movie. I read the paper some more.

"It is what you do," Susan said.

"Yeah."

"But it scares me," Susan said.

"Hell, it scares me too," I said.

CHAPTER

10

I was in Martin Quirk's office in Boston Police Headquarters on Boylston. Quirk's office overlooked Stanhope Street, which was much more of an alley than a street.

Quirk was wearing a beige corduroy jacket today, with a tattersall shirt and a maroon knit tie. His dark thick hair was cut very short and his thick hands were nicely manicured. He was sitting at his desk so I couldn't see his pants, but I knew they'd be creased and his shoes would gleam with polish and would match his belt. His desk was empty except for a picture of his wife, children, and dog.

"You are the neatest bastard I ever saw," I said. "Except maybe Hawk."

"So?" Quirk said.

"And the gabbiest."

Quirk didn't say anything. He merely sat, his hands quiet on the bare desk top.

"You called me," I said.

"How you doing on the killing outside Double Deuce?" Quirk said.

"We're hanging around awaiting developments," I said.

"And?"

"Hobarts have noticed us."

"And?"

"And nothing much. Kid named Major Johnson seems to run things."

"They make a run at you yet?"

"Nothing serious," I said.

Quirk nodded.

"Will be," Quirk said. "They buzz the kid and her baby?"

"Probably," I said. "They seem to be the force in Double Deuce."

"You doing any investigating or are you just sitting around scaring the Homies?"

"Mostly sitting," I said.

"Anybody in the project talk with you?"

"Nearly as much as they talk with you," I said.

Quirk nodded.

"Tillis got a line on anything?"

"He thinks I'm the white Satan."

"He thinks whatever will get his face on television," Quirk said. "Just happens to be right this time."

"Be more photo opportunities if the kids were white."

Quirk shrugged.

"You got any problem with us looking into this?" I said.

"No," Quirk said. "I hope you find out who did it and Hawk kills him. What's he doing in this?"

"Hard to say about Hawk," I said.

"We won't bother you," Quirk said. "I want someone to go down for killing the kid and her baby. We got the slugs. We can identify the gun if we find it."

"I know," I said. "Nine millimeter. I'll keep an eye out."

"Not hard to find on Hobart Street," Quirk said. "We can help, we will. Hawk wants to handle it his way, be fine with me."

"Me too," I said.

11

When Hawk picked me up in the morning there was a woman with him. She was stunning and black with a wide mouth and big eyes and her hair cut fashionably short. She wore a light gray suit with a short skirt. Even sitting in the car she was tall, and her thighs were noticeably winsome. I got in the back. Hawk introduced us. The woman's name was Jackie Raines. In her lap she held a briefcase.

"Jackie's going to sit with us today," Hawk said. He put the Jag in gear and we slid away from the curb in front of Susan's place and headed down Linnaean Street.

"Good," I said. "I was getting really sick of you."

"I'm a producer," Jackie said. "For *The Marge Eagen Show.*"

"Television?" I said.

"My God, yes," Jackie said. "It's the most successful local talk show in the country."

"Un huh," I said.

"Not a fan?" Jackie said.

"Mostly I only watch television if there's a ball involved, or maybe horses."

"Well, Marge wants to do a major, week-long, five-part series on the gangs in Boston," Jackie said. "And she spoke to me about it. She thought we'd be best to focus on an event related to one gang, in one locale. We knew of course about the murder and the problems at Double Deuce, so I spoke to Hawk."

"Of course," I said.

"I thought if anyone could help those people it would be Hawk, and I could tag along and get my story. And we could get it on in time for sweeps period."

I smiled.

"That sounds swell," I said. "Have you and Hawk known one another for long?"

"I've known Jackie most of my life," Hawk said.

Jackie put her hand lightly on his thigh.

"I hadn't seen Hawk for years, and then, after my divorce, I ran into him again."

"Gee whiz, Hawkster," I said. "You forgot to mention Jackie when you hired me to solve the murders and save all the poor folks at Double Deuce. How'd you happen to hear about the problems at Double Deuce, Jackie?"

"The local minister, man named Orestes Tillis," Jackie said. "He wants to be a state senator."

"Anyone would," I said. "So Hawk and I are going to clean up Double Deuce and you're going to cover it, and Marge Eagen is going to be able to charge more for commercial time on her show. And Rev Tillis will get elected."

"I know you're being cynical, but I guess, in fact, that's the truth. On the other hand, if you do clean up Double Deuce, it really will be good for the people there. Regardless of Marge Eagen or Orestes Tillis. And whoever killed that child and her baby . . ."

"Sure," I said.

"He's just mad," Hawk said, "because he likes to think he's a catcher in the rye."

"I'm disappointed that I didn't figure it out something was up."

"I don't follow this," Jackie said.

"Hawk seemed to be helping people for no good reason. Hawk doesn't do that."

"Except you," Hawk said.

"Except me," I said. "And Susan, and probably Henry Cimoli."

"Who's Susan?" Jackie said.

"She's with me," I said.

"I thought of money, or getting even, or paying something off. I never thought of you."

"Me?"

"He's doing it for you."

Jackie looked at Hawk. Her hand still rested quietly on his thigh.

"That why you're doing it, Hawk?" she said.

"Sure," Hawk said.

She smiled at him, as good a smile as I'd seen in a while—except for Susan's—and patted his thigh.

"That's very heartwarming," she said.

Hawk smiled back at her and put one hand on top of her hand as it rested on his thigh.

Good heavens!

CHAPTER

12

As soon as we pulled into the Double Deuce quadrangle the Reverend Tillis and a woman with short gray-streaked hair came out of the building. Tillis had on a dashiki over his suit today. The woman wore faded pink jeans and a Patriots sweatshirt. Hawk got out of the car as they approached. Neither of them looked at me.

"This is Mrs. Brown," Tillis said. "She has a complaint about the Hobarts."

Hawk smiled at her and nodded his head once.

"Go ahead," Tillis said to her.

"They been messing with my boy," the woman said. "He going to school and they take his books away from him and they take his lunch money. I saved out that lunch money and they took it. And one of them push him down and tell him he better get some protection for himself."

The woman put both hands on her hips as she talked and her face was raised at Hawk as if she were expecting him to challenge her and she was ready to fight back.

"Where's your son?" Hawk said.

She shook her head and looked down.

"Boy's afraid to come," Tillis said.

Hawk nodded.

"Which one pushed him down?"

The woman raised her head defiantly. "My boy won't say."

"You know where I can find them?" Hawk said.

"They hanging on the corner, Hobart and McCrory," she said. "That where they be hassling my boy."

Hawk nodded again. I got out of the car on Hawk's side. Jackie got out the other.

"What you planning on?" Tillis said to Hawk.

"I tell you how to write sermons?" Hawk said.

"I represent these people," Tillis said. "I got a right to ask."

"Sure," Hawk said. "You know Jackie, I guess."

Tillis nodded and put out his hand. "Jackie. Working on that show?"

"Tagging along," she said.

"Figure this is for us?" I said.

"See what we do," Hawk said. "Otherwise no point to it. It ain't exactly the crime of the century."

"Mrs. Brown, I think you and I should allow Hawk to deal with this," Reverend Tillis said, making it sound regretful. Hawk grinned to himself.

There was no one in sight as we walked across the project. Jackie stayed with us. I looked at Hawk. He made no sign. It was warm for April. Nothing moved. The sun shone down. No wind stirred. Jackie took a small tape recorder out of her shoulder bag.

Ahead of us was a loud radio. The sound of it came from a van, parked at the corner. A couple kids were sitting in the van with the doors open. Major leaned against a lamppost. The big kid that Hawk had nailed last time was standing near him. The others were fanned out around. There were eighteen of them. I didn't see any weapons. The music abruptly shut off. The sound of Jackie's heels was suddenly loud on the hot top.

Major smiled at us as we stopped in front of him. I heard Jackie's tape recorder click on.

"What's you got the wiggle for, Fro?" Major said. "She for backup?"

The kids fanned out around him laughed.

"Which one of you hassled the Brown kid?" Hawk said.

"We all brown kids here, Fro," Major said.

Again laughter from the gang.

Hawk waited. Still no sign of weapons. I was betting on the van. It had a pair of doors on the side that open out. One of them was open maybe six inches. It would come from there. I wasn't wearing a jacket. The gun on my hip was apparent. It didn't matter. They all knew I had one,

63

anyway. Hawk's gun was still out of sight under a black silk windbreaker he wore unzipped. That didn't matter either, they knew he had one too.

"What you going to do, Fro, you find the hobo that hassed him?" Major said.

"One way to find out," Hawk said.

Major turned and grinned at the audience. Then he looked at the big kid next to him.

"John Porter, you do that?"

John Porter said "Ya," which was probably half the things John Porter could say. From his small dark eyes no gleam of intelligence shone.

"There be your man, Fro," Major said. "Lass time you mace him, he say you sucker him. He ain't ready, he say."

Hawk grinned. "That right, John Porter?"

The cork was going to pop. There was no way that it wouldn't. Without moving my head I kept a peripheral fix on the van door.

John Porter said, "Ya."

"You ready now, John Porter?" Hawk said.

John Porter obviously was ready now. His knees were flexed, his shoulders hunched up a little. He had his chin tucked in behind his left shoulder. There was some scar tissue around his right eye. There was the scar along his jawline, and his nose looked as if it had thickened. Maybe boxed a little. Probably a lot of fights in prison.

"Care to even things up for the sucker punch?" Hawk said.

"John Porter say he gon whang yo ass, Fro," Major said. "First chance he get."

The laughter still skittered around the edges of everything Major said. But his voice was tauter now than it had
been.

"Right, John Porter?" Major said.

John Porter nodded. His eyes reminded me of the eyes
of a Cape buffalo I'd seen once in the San Diego Zoo. He
kept his stare on Hawk. It was what the gang kids called
mad-dogging. Hawk's grin got wider and friendlier.

"Well, John Porter," Hawk said, friendly as a Bible
salesman, "You right 'bout that sucker punch. And being as
how you a brother and all, I'll let you sucker me. Go on
ahead and lay one upside my head, and that way we start
out even, should anything, ah, develop."

John Porter looked at Major.

"Go on, John Porter, do what the man say. Put a charge
on his head, Homes."

John Porter was giving this some thought, which was
clearly hard for him. Was there some sort of trickery here?

"Come on, John Porter," Major said. "Man, you can't
fickle on me now. You tol me you going to crate this Thomp-
son first chance. You tol me that, Homes." In everything
Major said there was derision.

John Porter put out a decent overhand left at Hawk,
which missed. Hawk didn't seem to do anything, but the
punch missed his chin by a quarter of an inch. John Porter
had done some boxing. He shuffled in behind the left with
a right cross, which also missed by a quarter of an inch.
John Porter began to lose form. He lunged and Hawk
stepped aside and John Porter had to scramble to keep his
balance.

"See, the thing is," Hawk said, "you're in over your head, John Porter. You don't know what you are dealing with here."

John Porter rushed at Hawk this time, and Hawk moved effortlessly out of the way. John Porter was starting to puff. He wasn't quite chasing Hawk yet. He had enough ring savvy left to know that you could get your clock cleaned by a Boy Scout if you started chasing him incautiously. But chasing Hawk cautiously wasn't working. John Porter had been trained, probably in some jailhouse boxing program, in the way to fight with his fists. And it wasn't working. It had probably nearly always worked. He was 6'2" and probably weighed 240, and all of it muscle. He might not have lost a fight since the fourth grade. Maybe never. But he was losing this one and the guy wasn't even fighting. John Porter didn't get it. He stopped, his hands still up, puffing a little, and squinted at Hawk.

"What you doing?" he said.

Major stepped behind John Porter and kicked him in the butt.

"You fry him, John Porter, and you do it now," Major said.

There was no derision in Major's voice.

"He can't," Hawk said, not unkindly.

John Porter made a sudden sweep at Hawk with his right hand and missed. The side door of the van slid an inch and I jumped at it and rammed it shut with my shoulder on someone's hand, someone yelled in pain, something clattered on the street. I kept my back against the door and came up with the Browning and leveled it sort of inclusively at the group. Hawk had a left handful of John Porter's hair. He held John Porter's head down in front of him, and with his right hand, pressed the muzzle of a Sig Sauer automatic into John Porter's left ear. Jackie had dropped flat to the pavement and was trying with her left hand to smooth her skirt down over her backside, while her right hand pushed the tape recorder as far forward toward the action as she could.

Somewhere on the other side of McCrory Street a couple of birds chirped. Inside the truck someone was grunting with pain. I could feel him struggle to get his arm out of the door. A couple of gang members were frozen in midreach toward inside pockets or under jackets.

"Now this time," Hawk was saying, "we all going to walk away from this."

No one moved. Major stood with no expression on his face, as if he were watching an event that didn't interest him.

"Next time some of you will be gone for good," Hawk said. "Spenser, bring him out of the truck."

I kept my eyes on the gang and slid my back off the door. It swung open and a small quick-looking kid no more than fourteen, in a black Adidas sweatsuit, came out clutching his right wrist against him. In the gutter by the curb, below the open door, was an automatic pistol. I picked it up and stuck it in my belt.

"You all walk away from here, now," Hawk said. No one moved.

"Do what I say," Hawk said. There was no anger in his voice. Hawk pursed his lips as he looked at the gang members standing stolidly in place. Behind him Jackie was on her feet again, her tape recorder still running, some sand clinging to the front of her dress.

Hawk smiled suddenly.

"Sure," he said.

He looked at me.

"They won't leave without him," Hawk said.

I nodded. Hawk released his grip on John Porter's hair and Porter straightened. He walked away from Hawk with his head down.

"You fucked yourself," Major said without any particular emotion. "You dead, motherfucker."

"Not likely," Hawk said.

Major stood silently for a moment, looking at Hawk, then he looked at me.

"Enjoy yourself, slut," he said to Jackie. And his face broke into a wide smile.

Then he turned and nodded at the gang. They followed him, and in a moment they were gone and all there was, was the two birds across the street, chirping.

CHAPTER

13

We were back in Hawk's car. Jackie in back this time, Hawk and I in the front seat. Both of us had shotguns.

"Would you like to reprise all of that for me?" Jackie said.

"Kid's playing a game," Hawk said.

"The leader? Major?"

"Un huh."

"Well, could you explain the game?"

Hawk grinned back at her over his shoulder. "Un uh," he said.

"Well, I mean, is it turf?" Jackie said.

"Sure it's turf, but it's more," Hawk said.

"I didn't even understand half what he was saying,"
Jackie said.

"Gangs have their own talk," Hawk said.

"You didn't understand it either," Jackie said.

"Not all of it. Got the drift though."

"I wonder if he's trying to see how you'll act?" I said to
Hawk.

"He's heard of me?" Hawk said. Hawk considered everything genuinely. He had almost no assumptions.

"Maybe," I said. I looked at Jackie. "I don't want to hear
any of this on *The Marge Eagen Show*."

"No," Jackie said. "Unless I warn you, it's background
only. Okay?"

I nodded.

"Maybe Major has heard of you. Maybe you are a kind
of ghetto legend, like Connie Hawkins was on the New
York playgrounds, say, for different reasons. . . ."

"Who's Connie Hawkins?" Jackie said.

"Basketball player," Hawk said. He kept his eyes on me.
"Yeah?"

"So maybe Major wants to learn," I said.

Hawk nodded slowly and kept nodding.

"Learn how to handle trouble?" Jackie said.

"How a man behaves," Hawk said. He kept nodding.
"That's why they haven't just done a drive-by and sprayed
us."

"Which is not to say they won't," I said.

"But if he want to learn, he will escalate slow," Hawk
said.

70

"And observe, and if it goes right for him, maybe he can win over his father."

"Father?" Jackie said.

Hawk grinned again. "Spenser got a shrink for a girlfriend," he said. "Sometimes he get a little fancy."

"I try not to use any big words, though. I respect your limitations."

"Limitations?" Hawk said. "I got no limitations. Why you think I'm a ghetto legend?"

"Beats me," I said.

CHAPTER

14

"So what's she like?" Susan said.

We were having a supper, which I'd cooked, and sipping some Sonoma Riesling, in the kitchen of what Susan now insisted on calling "our house."

"Well, she's brave as hell," I said. "When the guns came out this morning, she hit the pavement facedown, but she kept her tape recorder going."

Susan moved some of her chicken cutlet about in the wine lemon sauce I had made.

"Smart?"

"I think so," I said. "She asks a lot of questions—but that is, after all, her job."

Susan cut a becomingly modest triangle of chicken, speared it with her fork, raised it to her lips, and bit off half of it. Pearl sat quietly with her head on Susan's thigh, her eyes fixed poignantly on the supper. Susan put the fork down and Pearl took the remaining bite quite delicately.

"There are dogs," I said, "who eat Gaines Meal from a bowl on the floor."

"There are dogs who are not treated properly," Susan said. "Is she attractive?"

"Jackie? Yeah, she's stunning."

"Is she the most stunning woman you know?" Susan said. She put her fork down and picked up her napkin from her lap. She patted her lips with it, put it back, picked up her wineglass, and drank some wine.

"She is not," I said, "as stunning as you are."

"You're sure?"

"No one is as stunning as you are," I said.

She smiled and sipped more of her wine.

"Thank you," she said.

I had cooked some buckwheat noodles to go with the chicken, and some broccoli, and some whole-wheat biscuits. We both attended to that, for a bit, while Pearl inspected every movement.

"Am I as stunning as Hawk?" I said.

Susan gazed at me for a moment without any expression. "Of course not," she said and returned to her food.

I waited. I knew she couldn't hold it. In a moment her shoulders started to shake and finally she giggled audibly. She raised her head, giggling, and I could see the way her eyes tightened at the corners as they always did when she was really pleased.

"You don't meet that many shrinks that giggle," I said.

"Or have reason to," Susan said as her giggling became sporadic. "What's for dessert?"

"I could tear off your clothes and force myself upon you," I said.

"We had that last night," Susan said. "Why can't we have desserts like other people—you know, Jell-O Pudding, maybe some Yankee Doodles?"

"You wouldn't say that if I was as stunning as Hawk," I said.

"True," Susan said. "Do you think he's serious about her?"

"What is Hawk serious about?" I said. "I've never known him before to bring a woman along when we were working."

"Well, is she serious about him?"

"She acts it. She touches him a lot. She looks at him a lot. She listens when he speaks."

"That doesn't mean eternal devotion," Susan said.

"No, some women treat every guy like that," I said. "Early conditioning, I suppose. But Jackie doesn't seem like one of them. I'd say she's interested."

"And he's taking on this gang for her," Susan said.

"Yeah, but that may be less significant than it seems," I said. "Hawk does things sometimes because he feels like doing them. There aren't always reasons, at least reasons that you and I would understand, for what he does."

"I agree that I wouldn't always understand them," Susan said. "I'm not so sure you wouldn't."

I shrugged.

"Whatever," I said. "He may have decided to do this just to see how it would work out."

Susan held her glass up and looked at the last of the sunset glowing through it from her west-facing kitchen windows.

"I would not wish to be in love with Hawk," Susan said.

"You're in love with me," I said.

"That's bad enough," she said.

15

Hawk parked the Jag parallel to Hobart Street in the middle of the project. It was a great April day and we got out of the car and leaned on the side of it away from the street. Jackie and her magic tape recorder were there, listening to the silence of the project.

"How come in books and movies the ghetto is always teeming with life: dogs barking, children crying, women shouting, radios playing, that sort of thing? And I come to a real ghetto, with two actual black people, and I can hear my hair growing?"

"Things are not always what they seem," Hawk said. He was as relaxed as he always was, arms folded on the roof

of the car. But I knew he saw everything. He always did.
"Oh," I said.

"This is the first ghetto I've ever been to," Jackie said. "I grew up in Hohokus, New Jersey. My father is an architect. I thought it would be like that too."

"Mostly in a place like this," Hawk said, "people can't afford dogs and radios. You can afford those, you can afford to get out. Here it's just people got no money and no power, and what kids they got they keep inside to protect them. People here don't want to attract attention. Somebody know you got a radio, they steal it. People want to be invisible. This place belongs to the Hobart Street Gang. They the only ones with radios. The only ones noisy."

"And we've quieted them down," I said.

"For the moment," Hawk said.

Jackie was standing between Hawk and me. She was leaning her shoulder slightly against Hawk's.

"Did you grow up in a place like this, Hawk?"

Hawk smiled.

A faded powder blue Chevy van pulled around the corner of Hobart Street and cruised slowly past us. Its sides were covered with graffiti. Hawk watched it silently as it drove past. It didn't slow and no one paid us any attention. It turned right at McCrory Street and disappeared.

"You think that was a gang car?" Jackie said.

"Some gang," Hawk said.

"Hobart?"

Hawk shrugged.

"So how do you know it's a gang van?" Jackie said.

77

"Nobody else would have one," Hawk said.

"Because they couldn't afford it?"

Hawk nodded. He was looking at the courtyard.

"Gang would probably take it away from anyone who wasn't a member," I said.

Jackie looked at Hawk.

"Is that right?" she said.

Hawk nodded.

"You can usually trust what he say," Hawk said. "He's not as dumb as most white folks."

"Does this mean we're going steady?" I said to Hawk.

He grinned, his eyes still watching the silent empty place. Cars passed occasionally on Hobart Street, but not very many. The sun was strong for this early in spring, and there were some pleasant white clouds here and there making the sky look bluer than it probably was. To the north I could see the big insurance towers in the Back Bay. The glass Hancock tower gleamed like the promise of Easter; the sun and sky reflected in its bright facing.

"Well, did you?" Jackie said.

"Don't matter," Hawk said.

Jackie looked at me.

"I grew up in Laramie, Wyoming," I said.

"And do you know where he grew up?" Jackie said.

"No."

Jackie took in a long slow breath and let it out. She shook her head slightly.

"God," she said. "Men."

"Can't live with them," I said. "Can't live without them."

78

Across the empty blacktop courtyard, out from between two buildings, Major Johnson sauntered as if he were walking into a room full of mirrors. He was in the full Adidas today, hightops, and a black warm-up suit, jacket half zipped over his flat bare chest. He wore his Raiders hat carefully askew, with the bill pointing off toward about 4 A.M. He was alone.

Hawk began to whistle through his teeth, softly to himself, the theme from *High Noon*. Between us, I could feel Jackie stiffen.

"How you all doing today?" Major said when he reached the car. He stood on the opposite side and rested his forearms on the roof as Hawk was doing. He was shorter than Hawk, and the position looked less comfortable.

Hawk had no reaction. He didn't speak. He didn't look at Major. He didn't look away. It was as if there were no Major. Major shifted his gaze to me. He was the first person who'd looked at me since I'd come to Double Deuce.

"How you doing, Irish?"

"How's he know I'm Irish?" I said to Hawk.

"You white," Hawk said.

"You call all white people Irish?" Jackie said. She had placed her tape recorder on the car roof.

"We gon be on TV?" Major said, looking at the tape recorder.

"Maybe," Jackie said. "Right now I'm just doing research."

"Goddamn," Major said. "I sure pretty enough to be on TV."

79

He turned his head in profile.

"You want to know 'bout my sad life?" he said.

"Anything you'd care to tell me," Jackie said.

"I don't care to tell you nothing, sly," Major said.

"I'm sorry you feel that way," Jackie said.

"I don't know no better, you understand. I is an under-privileged ghet-to youth."

"Mostly you are an asshole," Hawk said. He was looking at Major now. His voice had no emotion in it, just the usual pleasant inflection.

"Not a good idea to dis me, Fro," Major said. "You in my crib now."

"Not anymore," Hawk said. "Belongs to me."

"The whole Double Deuce, Fro? You been smoking too much grain. You head is juiced."

Hawk smiled serenely.

"Why you think you and the Flap can shut the Deuce down? Five-oh can't do it. Why you think you can?"

"We got nothing else to do," Hawk said.

Major grinned suddenly and patted the roof of the Jaguar.

"Like your ride," he said.

Jackie wasn't a quitter. "Can you tell me anything about being a gang member?" she said.

"Like what you want to know?"

"Well," Jackie said, "you are a member of a gang."

"I down with the Hobarts," he said.

"Why?"

Major looked at Jackie as if she had just questioned him about gravity.

80

"We all down," he said.

"Who's we?"

Again the look of incredulity. He glanced at Hawk.

"All the Homeboys," he said.

"What does membership in the gang mean?"

Major looked at Hawk again and shook his head.

"I'll see you all again," he said and turned and sauntered off into one of the alleys between the monolithic brick project buildings and disappeared. Hawk watched him until he was out of sight.

"I'm not sure it was fatherly to call him an asshole," I said.

"Honest, though," Hawk said.

"What was that all about?" Jackie said. "You guys are like his mortal enemy. Why would he come talk to you?"

"Ever read about Plains Indians?" Hawk said. "They had something called a coup stick and it was a mark of the greatest bravery to touch an enemy with it. Counting coup they called it. Not killing him, counting coup on him. That's what they'd brag about."

"Was that what Major was doing? Was he counting coup on you?"

Hawk nodded.

"More than that," I said. "To a kid like Major, Hawk is the ultimate guy. The one who's made it. Drives a Jag. Dresses top dollar—I think he looks pretty silly, but Major would be impressed—got a top-of-the-line girlfriend."

"Me? How would he know I was Hawk's girlfriend?"

"All you could be," Hawk said. His eyes were still resting on the alley where Major had disappeared. "In his

81

world there aren't any women who are television produ-
cers. There's mothers, grandmothers, sisters, aunts, and
girlfriends."

"For crissake—that defines women only in reference to
men," Jackie said.

"Ain't that the truth," Hawk said.

16

It was quarter to nine when I came into the house on Linnaean Street in Cambridge. Susan had her office and waiting room on the first floor; and she, and now I, lived upstairs. Pearl capered about and lapped my face when I came in, and Susan came from the kitchen and gave me a peck on the lips.

"Where you been?" she said.

"Double Deuce," I said.

I went past her to the kitchen. There were three bottles of Catamount beer in behind some cartons of low-fat lemon yogurt sweetened with aspartame. I got a bottle of beer out and opened it and drank from the bottle. On the stove, a pot of water was coming to a boil. I put the bottle down and tipped it a little and Pearl slurped a little beer from it.

"You don't like it when I ask where you've been," Susan said.

I shrugged.

"I don't mean it in any censorious way," Susan said.

"I know." I wiped the bottle mouth off with my hand and drank a little more beer. "I have lived all my life, nearly, in circumstances where I went where I would and did what I did and accounted to no one."

"Even as a boy?"

"My father and my uncles, once I was old enough to go out alone, didn't ask where I'd been."

"But two people who live with one another, who share a life . . . It is a reasonable question."

"I know," I said. "Which is why I don't say anything."

"But you do," Susan said. "Your whole body resents the question. The way you hold your head when you answer, the way you roll your shoulders."

"Betrayed," I said, "by my expressive body."

"I'm afraid so," Susan said.

She held her gaze on me. Her huge dark eyes were serious. Her mouth showed the little lines at the corner that showed only when she was angry.

"Suze, I've lived alone all my adult life. Now I'm cohabitating in a large house in Cambridge with a yard and a dog."

"You love that dog," Susan said.

"Of course I do. And I love you. But it is an adjustment."

She kept her gaze on my face another moment and then she smiled and put her hand on my cheek and leaned forward, bending from the waist as she always did, a perfect lady, and kissed me softly, but not hastily, on the mouth.

"I'm having pasta and broccoli for supper," she said. "Would you care for some?"

"No, thank you," I said. "I'll drink a couple of beers and then maybe make a sandwich or something and watch the Celtics game."

"Fine," Susan said.

She cut the tops off the broccoli and threw the stalks away. Then she separated the flowerets and piled them up on her cutting board. I sat on a stool opposite her and watched.

"You could peel those stalks and freeze them," I said. "Be great for making a nice soup when you felt like it."

Susan looked at me as if I had begun speaking in tongues.

"In my entire life," Susan said, "I have never, ever felt like making a nice soup."

Susan put some whole-wheat pasta in the pot, watched while it came back to a boil again, and tossed in her broccoli. It came to a second boil and she reached over and set the timer on her stove. While it cooked she tossed herself a large salad with some shaved carrots and slices of yellow squash and a lot of lettuce.

"Susan," I said, "you're cooking. I'm not sure I've ever seen you cooking."

85

"We've done a lot of cooking together," Susan said. "Holidays, things like that."

"Yeah. But this is just cooking supper," I said. "It's very odd to see you cooking supper."

"Actually I kind of like cooking for myself," Susan said. "I can have what I want and cook it the way I want to and not be subject to suggestions, or complaints, or derision— even if I throw away broccoli stalks."

"Actually I throw them away too," I said. "After I've peeled them and frozen them and left them in the freezer for a year."

"See," Susan said, "I've eliminated two steps in the process." She stirred her pasta and broccoli around once in the pot with a wooden spoon and got out a pale mauve plastic colander and put it in the sink.

"I have been talking to a woman I know who works with the gangs," she said.

"Oh?"

"She would be willing to talk with you. Not the television woman, just you. And Hawk if he wishes."

"Social worker?" I said.

Susan shook her head.

"No, she's a teacher. And after school she spends her time on the street. It's what she does. It's her life."

"She black?"

"No."

"And the kids tolerate her?"

"They trust her," Susan said. "You want to talk?"

"Sure," I said. "Pays to understand your enemy."

"She does not see them as the enemy," Susan said.

"She's not hired to protect people from them," I said.

"If you want her input," Susan said, "you should probably not stress that aspect."

"Good point," I said.

CHAPTER

17

Orestes Tillis was waiting for us when we arrived for work at Double Deuce the next day.

"They set twelve fires last night," he said.

Hawk nodded. Jackie clicked on her recorder.

"They set one in every trash can in the project," Tillis said. He glanced at Jackie's recorder. "And I believe I know why. It is an affront to every African-American that you should have one of the oppressors with you, protecting black people from each other."

Hawk nodded again.

"That's probably it," he said.

"You cannot be taken seriously as long as you appear allied with the oppressor," Tillis said.

"Sure," Hawk said.

"Are you saying that blacks and whites cannot work together?" Jackie said. Unconsciously she held the tape recorder forward. Tillis pointed it like a spaniel with a partridge.

"Could slaves work with slaveholders?" he said. "The white man is still trying to enslave us economically. He tries to destroy us with drugs and guns. Where does all the dope come from here? Do you see heroin labs in the ghetto? Do you see any firearms factories in the ghetto?"

Tillis pointed at me rather dramatically, considering that it was only us and the tape recorder.

"His people are practicing genocide, should we ask them for help?"

"You shut that thing off," Hawk said to Jackie, "and he'll shut up."

She looked startled, but she switched off the tape recorder. Tillis stopped gazing into it and looked at Hawk.

"They will not take you seriously," he said, "if you work with a white man."

Hawk stared at Tillis without expression for probably fifteen seconds. Then he shook his head slowly.

"You got it backwards," he said. "We the only thing they do take seriously. We all they can think about sitting out in the middle of their turf. They set those fires to see what we'd do. They don't care about you. We are an affront to them. They think about us all the time."

"Why don't they just shoot you?" Tillis said.

"Maybe one reason being they can't," Hawk said. "And maybe they kind of interested, see what we do."

"Why?"

"They admire Hawk," Jackie said.

Hawk continued as if neither of them had spoken.

"And they going to keep doing things, a little worse, and a little worse, and finally they going to get into shooting with us and we going to kill some of them."

Tillis' eyes shifted to Jackie and back to Hawk.

"Just like that?" he said.

"Un huh," Hawk said. "Maybe get lucky and one of the ones we kill will be the dude that did Devona and Crystal."

Tillis started to say "who?" and then remembered and caught himself.

"You sound like you are talking about simply shooting them to clean up the problem," he said.

"Un huh."

"I want no part of that," Tillis said. He glanced again at Jackie, who was all the media he had at the moment. "I can't condone murder."

Hawk shrugged.

"What makes you think they won't kill you?" Tillis said.

"Blue-eyed devil here," Hawk said, "going to prevent them."

"And I thought you'd never even noticed my eyes," I said.

CHAPTER

18

Erin Macklin came to my office at about 9:30 in the evening. She had thick dark hair cut short and salted with a touch of gray. Her features were even. Her makeup was understated but careful. She wore big horn-rimmed glasses, a string of big pearls, matching pearl earrings, a black suit, and a white blouse with the collar points worn out over the lapels of the suit. Her shoes were black, with medium heels. Dress for success. She looked around my office, located the customer's chair, and sat in it.

"I am here," she said, "because two people I know tell me Susan Silverman is to be trusted, and Susan Silverman says you can be trusted."

"One can't be too careful," I said.

"I also know a woman named Iris Milford who says she knew you nearly twenty years ago, and, at least at that time, you could leap tall buildings at a single bound."

"Iris exaggerates a little," I said becomingly. "When I knew her she was a student. How is she?"

"She has stayed in the community," Erin Macklin said. "She has made a difference."

"She seemed like she might," I said.

"You and another man are attempting to deal with the Hobart Street Raiders," she said.

"Actually," I said, "we *are* dealing with them."

"And Susan told me that you would like to know what I know about the gangs."

"Yes," I said. "But first I'd probably like to know a little about you."

"I was about to say the same thing," Erin Macklin said. "You first."

"I used to be a fighter. I used to be a cop. Now I am a private detective," I said. "I read a lot. I love Susan."

I paused for a moment thinking about it.

"The list," I said, "is probably in reverse order."

"A romantic," she said. "You don't look it."

I nodded.

"The man you are working with?"

"My friend," I said.

"Nothing more?"

"Lots more, but most of it I don't know."

"He's black," she said.

"Yes."

We were quiet while she looked at me. There was no challenge in the look, and the silence seemed to embarrass neither of us.

"I used to be a nun," she said. "Now I am a teacher at the Marcus Garvey Middle School on Cardinal Road. I teach a course titled the History of Contemporary America. When I began we had no books, no paper, no pencils, no chalk for the blackboard, no maps. This made for innovation. I started by telling them stories, and then by getting them to talk about the things that they had to talk about. And when what they said didn't shock me, and I didn't dash for the dean of discipline, they told me more about the things they knew. The course is now a kind of seminar on life for fourteen-year-old black children in the ghetto."

"Any books yet?"

"Yes. I bought them books," she said. "But they won't read them much. Hard to find books that have anything to do with them."

"*The March of Democracy* is not persuasive," I said.

She almost smiled.

"No," she said. "It is not persuasive."

She paused again, without discomfort, and looked at me some more. Her eyes were very calm and her gaze was steady.

"I used to work in day care, and we'd try to test some of the kids when they came in. The test required them, among other things, to draw with crayons. When we gave them to the kids they didn't know what the crayons were. Several tried to eat them."

"The test was constructed for white kids," I said.

"The test was constructed for middle-class kids," she said. "The basal reader family."

"Mom, Dad, Dick, and Jane," I said.

"And Spot," she said. "And the green tree."

"You and God have a lovers' quarrel?" I said.

Again she almost smiled.

"Gracious," she said. "A literate private eye."

"Anything's possible," I said.

"No. I had no quarrel with God. He just began to seem irrelevant. I could find no sign of Him in these kids' lives. And the kids' lives became more important to me than He did."

"The ways of the Lord," I said, "are often dark, but never pleasant."

"Adler?"

"Theodor Reik, I think."

She nodded.

"It also became apparent to me that they needed more than I could give them in class. So I stayed after school for them and then I began going out into the streets for them. Now I'm there after school until I get too sleepy, four or five days a week. I came from there now."

"Dangerous?" I said.

"Yes."

"But you get along."

"Yes."

"Is being white a handicap?"

She did smile. "Kids say I'm beige. Getting beiger."

"Save many?" I said.

"No."

"Worth the try," I said.

"One is worth the try," she said.

"Yes."

"You understand that, don't you?" she said.

"Yes."

She nodded several times, sort of encouragingly. She leaned back a little in her chair, and crossed her legs, and automatically smoothed her skirt over her knees. I liked her legs. I wondered for a moment if there would ever be an occasion, no matter how serious, no matter who the woman, when I would not make a quick evaluation when a woman crossed her legs. I concluded that there would never be such an occasion, and also that it was a fact best kept to myself.

"A while back the state decided to train some women to work with the kids in the ghetto. The training was mainly in self-effacement. Don't wear jewelry, don't bring a purse, don't wear makeup, move gingerly on the street, don't make eye contact. Be as peripheral as possible."

She shook her head sadly.

"If I behaved that way I'd get nowhere. I make eye contact. I say *hi*. Not to do that is to *dis* them. If you *dis* them they retaliate."

"*Dis* as in disrespect," I said.

"Yes. The thing is that, to the people training the women, these kids were an hypothesis. They didn't know them. Everything is like that. It's theory imposed on a

95

situation, rather than facts derived from it. You understand?"

"Sure," I said. "It's deductive, and life is essentially
inductive. Happens everywhere."

"But here, with these kids, when it happens it's lethal.
They are almost lost anyway. You can't afford the luxury of
theory. You have to know."

"And you know," I said.

"Yes," she said. "I know. I'm there every day, alone, on
my own, without a theory. I listen, I watch. I work at it. I
don't have an agenda. I don't have some vision of what the
truth ought to be."

She was alive with the intensity of her commitment.

"Nobody knows," she said. "Nobody knows what those
kids know, and until you do, and you're there with them,
you can't do anything but try to contain them." She paused
and stared past me out the dark window.

"Had one of my kids on probation," she said. "Juvie
judge gave him a nine P.M. curfew and he kept missing it.
There was a drug dealer, used to work the corner by the
kid's house every night. So I got him to keep an eye on the
kid, and every night he'd make sure the kid was in by
nine."

She smiled. "You got to know," she said.

"And if you do know," I said, "and you are there, how
many can you save?"

She took in a long slow breath and let it out through her
nose.

"A few," she said.

The overhead light was on, as well as my desk lamp, and the room was quite harsh in the flat light of it. I had the window cracked open behind me, and there was enough traffic on Berkeley and Boylston streets to make a sporadic background noise. But my building was empty except for me, and Erin Macklin, and its silence seemed to overwhelm the occasional traffic.

19

I kept two water glasses in the office. In case someone were overcome with emotion, I could offer them a glass of water, or if they became hysterical I could throw water in their face. I also kept a bottle of Irish whiskey in the office, and Erin Macklin and I were using the water glasses to sip some of the Irish whiskey while we talked.

"A little kid," she said, "goes to the store. He has to cross somebody else's turf. Means he has to sneak. In a car he has to crouch down. The amount of energy they have to expend simply to survive . . ." She paused and looked down into her whiskey. She swirled it slightly in the bottom of the water glass.

"They live in anxiety," she said. "If they wear the wrong

color hat; if their leather jacket is desirable, or their sneakers; if they have a gold chain that someone wants; they are in danger. One out of four young men in the inner city dies violently. These kids are in a war. They have combat fatigue."

"And they're mad," I said.

I had shut the overhead light off, and the room was lit like *film noir*, with my desk lamp and the ambient light from the streets casting elongated vertical shadows against the top of my office walls and spilling their long black shapes onto my ceiling. I felt like Charlie Chan.

"Yes," she said. "They are very angry. And the only thing they can do with that anger, pretty much, is to harm each other over trivial matters."

She took in some of her whiskey. She sat still for a moment and let it work.

"Something has to matter," I said.

"Yes," she said. "That's exactly right."

"Are there turf issues?" I said.

"Sure, but a lot of the extreme violence grows out of small issues between individuals. Who *dissed* who. Who looked at my girl, who stepped on my sneaker."

"Something's got to matter."

"You get it, don't you," she said. "I didn't expect you would. I figured you'd be different."

"It has always seemed to me that there's some sort of inverse ratio between social structure and, what . . . honor codes? Maybe a little highfaluting for the issue at hand, but I can't think of better."

"By honor do you mean inner-directed behavior? Because these kids are not inner directed."

"No, I know they're not. I guess I mean that nature hates a vacuum. If there are no things which are important, then things are assigned importance arbitrarily and defended at great risk. Because the risk validates the importance."

Erin Macklin sat back in her chair a little. She was holding her whiskey glass in both hands in her lap. She looked at my face as if she were reading directions.

"You're not just talking about these kids, are you?" she said.

"Any of them got families?" I said. "Besides the gang?"

"Not always, but sometimes," she said.

Outside a siren whooped: fire, ambulance, cops. If you live in any city you hear sirens all the time. And you pay no attention. It's an environmental sound. Like wind and birdsong in the country. Neither of us reacted.

"Often the families are dysfunctional because of dope or booze or pathology. Sometimes they are abusive, the kind you see on television. But sometimes they are Utopian— my kid can do no wrong. My kid is fine. The other ones are bad. It's the myth by which the parent reassures herself, or occasionally himself, that everything is okay. And of course it isn't and the pressure on the kid to be the source, so to speak, of 'okayness' for the family adds to his stress and drives him to the gang. Sometimes the kid is the family caretaker. He's the one putting food on the table—usually from dealing drugs—nobody asks him where he got the money. He's valued for it." She raised her glass with both hands from her lap and drank some more of the whiskey.

"If you're dealing," she said, "you have to be down with the gang where you're dealing."

I stood and went around my desk and poured a little more whiskey into her glass. She made no protest. She had settled back into her chair a little; she seemed in a reverie as she talked about what was obviously her life's work.

"Then there's the other myth. The bad-seed myth. The family that tells the kid he's bad from birth. One of my kids got shot in the chest and was dying of it. I was there, and his mother was there. 'I told him he was no good,' she said to me. 'I told him he'd end up with a bullet in him before he was twenty. And I was right.' "

"What a triumph for her," I said.

The whiskey seemed to have no effect on her, and she drank like one who enjoyed whiskey—not like someone who needed it. She smiled, almost dreamily.

"Had a kid, about fifteen, named Coke. Smart kid, had a lot of imagination, felt a lot of things. He knew the numbers, one in four, and he was sure he was going to be the one. So, because he was certain he'd die young, he set out to impregnate as many girls as he could. Even had a schedule set up, so he could achieve the maximum possible pregnancies before he died."

"There'll be one child left to carry on," I said.

"Unfortunately there are twenty or thirty children left to carry on. All of them with junior high school girls for mothers, and no father."

"Did he die young?"

101

"Not yet," she said. "But he's not around for those children."

"They were a stay against confusion," I said.

"A continuation, a kind of self," she said, "that would survive him when the world he lived in overwhelmed him."

"And he never identified with the three out of four that don't die violently in youth," I said.

"No. The life's too hard for that kind of optimism."

"Seventy-five percent is good odds in blackjack," I said. "But for dying, it would not seem a source of much comfort."

"Where I work," she said, "there is no source of much comfort."

"Except maybe you," I said.

She smiled a little and sipped a little more whiskey.

"Isn't it pretty to think so," she said.

"Well," I said, "a literate ex-nun."

"Anything's possible," she said.

CHAPTER

20

"Are you going to do anything about them setting the fires?" Jackie said.

Hawk shook his head. We were back in the Double Deuce quadrangle looking at nothing.

"Why not?" Jackie said.

"Trivial," Hawk said.

"But it's a challenge, isn't it?"

"Not if we not challenged," Hawk said.

We were quiet. Nothing moved in Double Deuce. The sun was steady. There was no wind and the temperature was in the sixties.

Jackie sighed.

"Are you familiar with the word *enigmatic?*" she said.

"Un huh," Hawk said. He was looking at the empty courtyard just as if there were something to see.

"How about the word *uncommunicative?*"

Hawk grinned and didn't speak.

"Hawk, I'm not just asking to be nosy. I'm a reporter, I'm trying to work."

He nodded and turned his head to look at her. She was in the front seat beside him.

"What would you like to know?" he said.

"Everything," she said. "Including answers to questions I don't know enough to ask."

"That's a lot," Hawk said.

"Between strangers, yes," Jackie said. "Among casual acquaintances, even friends, yes. But I am under the impression that we are more than that."

"Un huh," Hawk said.

I was in the backseat, sitting crosswise with my legs stretched out as much as you can stretch legs out in the backseat of a Jaguar sedan. I had found a way to sit so that my gun didn't dig into my back, and I was at peace.

"Is that impression accurate?" Jackie said.

"Yes," Hawk said.

"Then for Christ sake why don't you, goddamn it, talk?"

"Jackie," Hawk said, "you think there's a plan. You'd have a plan. Probably do. So you ask questions like there was some plan at work. In the kind of work I do, there is no plan. Reason we so good at this work is we know it."

When he said "we" he moved his head slightly in my direction so she'd know who "we" was.

"So how do you decide?" Jackie said. "Like now, how do you decide that you won't respond to the trash fires?"

"Same way I decided that you and I be more than friends," Hawk said. "Seem like the right thing to do."

"I had something to do with deciding that," Jackie said.

"Sure," Hawk said.

"So you have a feeling that it's best to let the trash fires slide?" Jackie said.

Hawk looked at me.

"Jump in anytime you like," he said.

"I was just congratulating myself on not being in on this," I said.

Jackie turned in her seat. Her lipstick was very bright, and she had on a carmine blouse open at the throat. She looked like about twenty-two million dollars. *More than friends,* I thought. *Hawk, you devil.*

"You too?" she said. "What's wrong with you people, don't you talk?"

"Most people are grateful," I said.

"Jesus Christ," she said. "You are just like him, a master of the fucking oblique answer."

Hawk and I were silent for a moment.

"It's not willful," I said. "It's that very often we don't know how to explain what we know. We tend to think from the inside out. We tend to feel our way along. And because of the way we live it is more important usually to know what to do than to know how we know it."

"God—I thought that was the woman's rap," Jackie said. "Creatures of feeling. I thought men were supposed to be reasonable."

"I wouldn't generalize about men and women," I said. "But I don't think Hawk or I are operating on emotional whim. It's just the way we experience things sometimes needs to get translated sort of promptly into a, ah, course of action. So we have tended to bypass the meditative circuit."

"Wow," Hawk said.

I nodded. "I kind of like that myself," I said. "And going back afterwards and filling in feels like kind of a waste of time."

"Because the consequences of your actions will prove if you were right," Jackie said.

"Ya," I said.

Hawk nodded. He smiled happily.

"Is it intuition?" Jackie said.

"No, it's the sort of automatic compilation of data without thinking about it, and comparing it with other data previously recorded," I said. "Most of it sort of volition-less."

"The thing with these kids," Hawk said, "they want to see what I do, or Major does, and he seems to be the one calls the plays, because they want to know who we are and what we're like."

"Because of you," Jackie said.

"Un huh. And if they can get us to chase around after them for a misdemeanor like setting trash fires we going to look like fools. What do we do about it? Do we shoot them? For torching trash barrels? Do we slap them around? How do we know who did it?"

"So you let them get away with it?"

"Sure," Hawk said. "We ignore it. We're above it."

"You know those junior high school principals," I said, "who suspend students for stuff like wearing Bart Simpson Tee-shirts?"

"Yes," Jackie said. "They make themselves look like jerks."

I nodded. Hawk nodded. Jackie smiled. And she nodded.

"I get it," she said. "Why didn't you say that in the first place?"

Hawk and I were both silent for a moment.

"We didn't know it," Hawk said, "in the first place."

21

Jackie and Hawk and I were savoring some chicken fajita subs that Hawk had bought us on Huntington Ave., when Marge Eagen rolled up in a NewsCenter 3 van with her driver, her secretary, a soundwoman, and a cameraman. Two Housing Authority cops parked their car behind the van. A car from the Boston Housing Authority with three civilians in it parked behind the cops.

"Marge always likes to make a site visit," Jackie said to us. "She's very thorough."

"Inconspicuous, too," I said.

The Housing Authority cops got out and looked around. The civilians got out and grouped near the van. The driver got out and opened the van doors. The secretary got out of the back. The cameraman and the soundwoman got out of the front. And then Marge Eagen stepped out into the sunlight. The civilians stood a little straighter. The cops looked at her. One of them said something under his breath to the other one. They both looked like they wanted to laugh, but knew they shouldn't. Marge stopped with one foot on the ground and one foot still in the van. A lot of her leg showed. The cameraman took her picture.

"Good leg," I said to Hawk.

"From here," Hawk said.

"Her legs are very good," Jackie said. "And she wants the world to know it. Don't you ever watch?"

"No," I said.

Hawk shook his head.

"It's the trademark opening shot every day. Low shot, her with a hand mike, sitting on a high stool, key lit, legs crossed. Tight skirt."

The cameraman finished. Marge Eagen finished stepping from the van and strode across toward us. Everyone in Boston knew her. She was a television fixture. Blonde hair, wide mouth, straight nose, and an on-camera persona that resonated with compassion. I had never actually watched her show, but she was legendarily intense and caring and issue-oriented. Jackie got out of the car. Hawk and I didn't.

"Jackie," she said. "How bleak."

Her voice had a soft husky quality that made you think of perfume and silk lingerie. At least it made me think of

109

that, but Susan had once suggested that almost everything did.

"Her voice make you think of perfume and silk lingerie?" I said to Hawk.

He shook his head.

"Money," he said.

"Everything makes you think of that," I said.

"Are these the two centurions?" Marge Eagen said. She bent forward and looked in the car at us. She had on a black silk raincoat open over a low-cut ruffled blouse that looked like a man's tuxedo shirt. While she was bent over looking in at us, I could see that she was also wearing a white bra with lace trim, probably a C cup.

Jackie introduced us.

"Step out," Marge said, "so we can get a picture of you."

"No picture," Hawk said.

"Oh come on, Hawk," Marge said. "We need it for interior promo. This is going to be the biggest series ever done on local."

Hawk shook his head. Marge pretended not to see him. With a big smile she opened the car door.

"In fact I suspect it's going to show up on network. Just the idea circulating has got the network kiddies on the horn already. Don't be shy," she said. "Crawl out of there. Let's get that handsome *punim* on film."

Hawk stepped lazily out of the car. He looked past Marge Eagen to the cameraman.

"If you take a picture of me," he said, "I will take your camera away and hit you with it."

He looked steadily at the cameraman, who was a

friendly-looking little guy with a receding hair which he concealed by artful combing. He stepped back a full step under the impact of Hawk's stare and glanced quickly at the two Housing cops.

"Oh, stop the nonsense," Marge Eagen was saying. "Don't be—"

Hawk shifted his gaze to her. There was something in his eyes, though his face seemed entirely still. She stopped in midsentence, and while she didn't step back, she seemed somehow to recede a little. Jackie stepped slightly between them as if she weren't aware she was doing it.

"We want pictures of Marge really, Harry. That's the big thing. Against the background of the buildings, looking at them, gazing down an alley. Pointing maybe, while she talks with Mr. Albanese."

Harry nodded and began looking at the light. Marge Eagen sort of snorted and walked away with him. The soundwoman followed.

"Why couldn't you let him take a picture, for God's sake?" Jackie said under her breath.

"Rather not," Hawk said pleasantly.

"That's no reason," Jackie said and turned as the suits from the Housing Authority approached. "Sam Albanese, Jim Doyle," she said and introduced us. "I'm afraid I don't know your name," she said to the third guy.

"John Boc," he said. "Authority Police Force." He didn't offer to shake hands.

"Oh, sure." Jackie was jollier than the hostess at a sock hop. "You're the Chief, of course."

"This isn't the time," Albanese said. "But we don't ap-

111

preciate a couple of hired thugs trying to do our job for us. It's vigilante-ism."

"Actually," I said, "vigilante-ism would be if the residents banded together to do your job for you. This is more like consulting-ism, I think."

"We the Arthur D. Little," Hawk said, "of hired thugdom."

"Go ahead," Albanese said, "be funny. I've asked our counsel"—he nodded at Mr. Doyle, who was looking at us sternly—"to see if there may not be some violation of statute here."

Jackie clicked her tape recorder on very quietly while Albanese was talking. But he heard it. He was the kind of guy who spent his life listening for the click of tape recorders and the hum of a television camera.

Without breaking stride he said, "I think what Ms. Eagen is doing will be a major television event, and I can tell you here and now that every resource of my office will be at your disposal. Gangs are the scourge of public housing. The few bad kids give a lot of decent hardworking citizens a bad name."

"And drank rapidly a glass of water," I said.

"Excuse me?" Albanese said.

"A literary allusion," I said, "e.e. cummings."

"Don't know him," Albanese said.

I smiled politely.

We all stood without anything to say for a while and watched Marge being filmed. When they were through, she came back over to us. Harry took some film of her with

Albanese. The soundwoman followed along behind although no one was talking and as far as I could see there was no sound to record.

Then it was our turn again. Marge was going to charm us. She gave us a very big smile and the full force of her large blue eyes.

"Now," she said, "what are we to do with you gentlemen?"

"We could go bowling," I said. "And maybe a pizza after?"

She shook her head the way a parent does to a willful child.

"We'd like you to be in this piece," she said. "Both of you."

Hawk and I remained calm.

"This series will make a real contribution to the most disadvantaged among us," she said. "I'd like to get your slant on it, two men who have bridged the racial gulf and are teamed up to try and help others bridge it."

Hawk turned his head and looked over his shoulder. Then he looked back at Marge Eagen.

"You reading that off something?" he said.

"You don't believe in what you're doing?" she said.

Up close I could see the small crowsfeet around her eyes. It didn't hurt her appearance. In some ways I thought it helped, made her look like a grown-up.

"I don't believe much," Hawk said, "and one of the things I don't believe is that some broad in a Donna Karan dress gonna do much to liberate the darkies."

113

"Well," Marge Eagen said, "there's no need to be offensive."

"Hell there ain't," Hawk said.

Marge Eagen said, "Jackie," and jerked her head at the van, did a brisk about-face, and marched away. Everybody except Boc, the Authority Police Chief, hustled after her. Hawk and I watched them silently.

"Don't pay attention to Albanese," Boc said. "We need all the help we can get down here, and if you can keep these fucking maggots quiet, you're not going to get any shit from us."

Hawk nodded. He was still looking after Marge.

"Good to know," he said.

Boc turned and went after the rest of them.

After maybe five minutes Jackie came back from the van. Her face was very tight.

"You asshole," she said to Hawk. "She's yanking me out of here. I don't even know if we're going to do the series."

Hawk nodded. Jackie got her purse out of Hawk's car, put her tape recorder in it, and went back to the van. She got in the van. It started up and pulled away. The Housing Authority car and the police car followed and Hawk and I were alone again in the middle of Double Deuce.

We looked at each other.

"How'd you know it was a Donna Karan dress," I said.

114

22

"Did you let her eat that bone on the couch?" Susan said.

It was 9:30 at night. I was reading *Calvin and Hobbes* in the morning edition of the *Globe*.

"Yeah," I said.

"Why didn't you stop her?"

"I didn't notice," I said. "Besides, why shouldn't she eat a bone on the couch?"

"Because she gets bone juice all over my cushions," Susan said. "How could you not notice?"

Answering questions like that had never proven fruitful. So I smiled ruefully and gave my head a beguiling twist and started back to *Calvin and Hobbes*. Then I would move to

Tank McNamara, and finish with *Doonesbury.* I had my evening all planned out.

"It is not funny," Susan said.

"No," I said, "that was a rueful smile."

"I'm serious," she said. "My stuff means a lot to me."

"I thought it was our stuff," I said.

"You know what I mean. I care about it. You don't."

"I know," I said. "I know that a lot of you goes into design and decor. It is part of your art. And the results are in fact artful. It's just that preventing the dog getting bone juice on your cushions was sort of on the back burner. I was feeling like I could read the paper and relax my vigilance for a bit."

"You were reading the comics," Susan said and walked out of the living room. I looked at Pearl, she did not seem abashed. She was vigorously getting bone juice on the rug.

23

I was in my office evaluating the health hazard of a third cup of coffee, compounded by the possibility of a donut. Outside my window it was overcast with the hard look of rain toward the river. A good day for coffee and donuts.

My office door opened, and there, radiant in a white raincoat and matching hat with a lot of blue polka dot showing at her neck, was Marge Eagen herself, the host of the number-one-rated local show in the country. My heart beat faster.

"Hello," I said.

"I wasn't sure whether to knock or not," Marge Eagen

said. She smiled beautifully. "I thought you might have a receptionist."

"I did," I said, "but she returned to her first love, neurosurgery, a while back and I haven't bothered to replace her."

Marge Eagen laughed delightedly.

"I heard you were funny," she said.

"Lot of people say that."

"May I sit down?"

"Of course," I said.

I nodded at the chair. She sat and glanced around my office.

"Great location," she said.

I didn't comment.

"Is it as fascinating as it seems," Marge Eagen said, "being a private detective?"

"Better than working," I said.

"Oh, I'm sure," she said, "that you work pretty damned hard."

"So what can I do for you?" I said.

"My, my," she said. "So businesslike."

She had unbuttoned her shiny white raincoat and let it fall off her shoulders over the back of the chair. She had on a dark blue dress with big white polka dots. When she crossed her legs, she showed me a lot of thigh. I remained calm.

"I really need to know what the problem is," Marge Eagen said.

I nodded encouragingly.

118

"Just what is the issue with your black friend," Marge said. "We're out there trying to do a story that should help his people, and, frankly, he seems to have a real attitude."

"Hawk?" I said. "An attitude?"

"Oh, come now, don't be coy, Mr. Spenser. What is his problem?"

"Why not consult with him?" I said.

"Well, I don't know where to find him, and in truth I'm more comfortable talking with you."

"Is it because I'm so cuddlesome?" I said.

She smiled the smile that launched a thousand commercials.

"Well, that's certainly part of it," she said.

"And I'm not a surly nigger," I said. "That's probably appealing too."

"There's no need to be coarse," Marge Eagen said. "The stations are really behind this. We believe in the project. We care."

"Hawk probably thinks you are a self-important ninny who is looking for television ratings and using the problems of the ghetto to that end. Hawk probably thinks that your coverage will do no good, and will make people think it's doing good, thus making things, if possible, worse."

Marge Eagen's face got red.

"You arrogant fucking prick," she said.

"Everyone says that," I said.

She stood, and turned, angrily shrugging her coat back on.

119

"Of course maybe he just doesn't like having his picture taken," I said. "With Hawk you never know."

She didn't answer. Without looking back she stalked out my door and slammed it shut behind her.

No business like show business.

24

It was raining when Major Johnson showed up with what appeared to be the whole Hobart posse. It was a light rain, and sometimes it would stop for a while and then pick up again, and the weather was warm. On the whole it was a nice rainy spring afternoon.

The Hobarts came down the alley from the back end of the project in single file. They all had on Raiders caps and Adidas sneakers. Most of them were in sweatsuits. Major had on a leather jacket with padded shoulders and a lot of zippers. As they came Hawk and I got out of the car to face them. I had the shotgun.

The Hobarts fanned out in a semicircle around us. I

didn't see John Porter. I took a look along the rooftops and saw nothing. Major stood inside the half-circle opposite us. He had the same half-amused, half-tense quality I had seen before.

"How you doing," Major said.

Hawk nodded slightly.

"Thought I should introduce you to the crew," Major said.

Hawk waited.

"Figure you suppose to be scrambling with us, you ought to see who you gonna have to hass."

There was still no movement on the roofline. The rain misted down softly, and no one seemed to mind it. The boys stood arrayed.

"This here is Shoe," Major said, "and Honk, Goodyear, Moon-man, Halfway, Hose."

At each name Hawk would shift his eyes onto the person introduced. He made no other sign. Shoe was the kid I'd yanked out of the van. Goodyear looked like he'd been named for the Blimp. Honk was very light. Halfway was very short. Major moved slowly around the semicircle.

"This here is X, and Bobby High."

I kept watching the roof, alternating glances at the street. The rain came a little harder.

". . . and Junior," Major said. "And Ray . . ."

There were maybe twenty kids in all. Major was around twenty. The youngest looked to be twelve or thirteen.

"Where's John Porter?" Hawk said.

Major shrugged. "He ain't here," Major said. "I think

maybe he soaking his hose." He grinned. "John Porter heavy on soaking it. Say he need to soak it every day since he got out of rails, you know? Say his slut spend most of her time looking at the ceiling."

"You come to tell me about John Porter's sex life?" Hawk said.

"Come to see you, Fro. Come to intro the Homes. You ever been in rails, Fro?"

Hawk said, "It's raining. You want to stand around in the rain?"

"We used to standing around," Major said. "Stand around a lot. Stand around sell some sub. Stand around pick up some wiggle, stand around throat a little beverage. Maybe trace somebody."

"Trace?" I said.

Major grinned. "You know, line somebody, haul out you nine and . . ." With his thumb and forefinger he mimicked shooting a handgun.

"Ah," I said. "Of course."

"What kind of sub you sell?" Hawk said.

"Grain, glass, classic, Jock, motor, harp, what you need is what we got."

Hawk looked at me. "Grass," he said. "Rock cocaine, regular powdered coke, heroin." He looked at Major. "What's motor? Speed?"

"Un huh."

"And PCP," Hawk finished.

"You think I didn't know that?" I said.

"What do you use?" Hawk said.

"We don't use that shit, man. You think we use that? We see what it does to people, man. We ain't stupid."

"So what do you use?" Hawk said.

"Beverage, Fro. I already tol you that. Some Mogen, some Juke, hot day maybe, some six. You use something?"

"I drink the blood of my enemies," Hawk said and smiled his wide happy smile. His eyes never left Major.

"Whoa," Major said. "That is dope, man!" He turned toward the others. "Is this a fresh dude? Did I tell you he was bad? The blood of the fucking enemies—shit!"

"How many people you lined?" Shoe asked Hawk.

Hawk looked at him as if he hadn't spoken.

"I killed me a Jeek, last month," Shoe said. "Mother-fucker tried to stiff me on a buy and I nined him right there." Shoe nodded toward the barren blacktop play-ground across the street. There were iron swing sets without swings, and a half-moon metal backboard with no hoop. The metal was shiny in the rain, and the blacktop gleamed with false promise.

"Doing much business since we here?" Hawk said.

"Do business when we want to," Major said.

"Who's your truck?" Hawk said.

Major looked at me for a minute and back at Hawk.

"Tony Marcus," he said proudly.

Hawk smiled even more widely.

"Really," he said.

"You know him?" Major said.

"Un huh," Hawk said. "My associate here once punched him in the mouth."

The entire semicircle was silent for a moment. For all

their ferocity they were kids. And a man who had punched Tony Marcus, and survived, got their attention.

"You do that?" Major said.

"He annoyed me," I said.

"I don't believe you done that," Major said.

I shrugged.

We were quiet for a while standing in the rain.

"Where the sly?" Major said. "She don't like us no more?"

"Why should she be different?" Hawk said.

"This mean we not going to be on TV?"

Hawk was quiet for a moment. He looked at Major while he was being quiet.

"We need to talk," Hawk said finally.

"What the fuck we doing, man?"

"Now, right now, you're profiling," Hawk said. "And I'm being bored."

"You bored, man, whyn't you put your motherfucking ass someplace else, then?"

"Why don't you and me sit in the car, out of the rain, and we talk?" Hawk said.

You could tell that Major liked that—he and Hawk as equals, the two commanders conferring while the troops stood in the rain. Besides, it was a Jaguar sedan with leather upholstery.

"No reason to get wet," Major said.

Hawk opened the back door and Major got in. Hawk got in after him. He grinned at me as he got in. I stayed outside the car, with the shotgun, staring at about nineteen hostile gangbangers, in the rain, which was coming harder.

125

25

We were at the other end of life. Susan and I and Hawk and Jackie were sharing a bottle of Iron Horse champagne and having dinner on the top floor of the Bostonian Hotel. Hawk had on a black silk suit and a white shirt with a pleated front. I was wearing my dark blue suit, which I almost always wore, because it flattered my eyes, and because I didn't have another one. I was sure we didn't look like people who spent their days sitting with guns in the middle of a housing project. And the women we were with didn't look like they'd date such people.

Jackie was wearing a little black dress with pearls. She rested her forearm on the back of Hawk's chair and traced small circles between his shoulder blades with her forefinger.

"You talked with the boy?" she said. "Actually talked?"

"Un huh."

"And are you going to tell me what he said?"

"Background only," Hawk said.

Jackie nodded.

"You notice," I said to Susan, "that the Kingfish accent seems to go away when he talks to Jackie?"

Susan smiled, which is something to see.

"Yes," she said, "but I am far too delicate to mention it."

"That is mostly for you honkies," Hawk said in a kind of David Niven accent, "so as not to confound your expectations."

"What did you and Major talk about?" Jackie said.

"Woman is not easily distracted," Hawk said.

"As you have every reason to know," Jackie said.

"I wasn't talking about that," Hawk said.

There was a moment of silence while Jackie smiled at him and Hawk gave her the same kindly look that he gave everyone.

"Major got in the car," Hawk said, "and I said to him, 'We can go two ways. We can talk, and work out an arrangement, or we can pop the cork on this thing.' Major looking mostly at the car while I'm talking. And when I say that, he sort of nod and keep looking at the car. And I say, 'I will kill you if I need to.' And he stop looking at the car and he sort of laugh."

"Really intimidated," I said.

ROBERT B. PARKER

"Yuh. He must know your reputation, too, 'cause he say
I be dead and the Mickey, which is you, be dead long time
ago, except he says no."

"We've had two encounters and come out first both
times," I said. "Doesn't that tell him anything?"

"No shooting," Hawk said. "Kids only impressed with
shooting. Everybody got a gun. What you and I would
punch somebody on the chops for, these kids shoot you."

"Makes you nostalgic for street fighters," I said.

Hawk nodded.

"Mickey?" Susan said.

"Irish," Hawk said, "means white."

"All whites?" Susan said.

"Un huh."

"Would I be Irish?" she said.

"You'd be slut, or sly, or wiggle," Hawk said. "Women's
race don't matter."

"Sexism again," Susan said.

"You might be an Irish slut, though," I said.

"Gee," Susan said, "my chance to pass."

"Make you an IAP," I said.

"There's no such thing," Susan said.

Hawk had some champagne. He drank it the way people
drink Pepsi-Cola. I had never seen it change him. Actually
I had never seen anything change him.

"I ask him why he hasn't given the word already, and he
say he trying to give me some respect, 'cause everybody
know 'bout me."

"Everybody?" Jackie said.

128

"He mean everybody on Hobart Street," Hawk said.

"Which to him is everybody," I said.

"Say everybody wondering why I am there with a flap," Hawk said and nodded at me. "They trying to figure that out. And he say, why am I? And I tell him it seem like a good idea at the time. He doesn't like the answer, so he sit a minute and he think about it. And then he say, 'So what you going to do?' And I say they can do what they want to do somewhere else, not my problem. I say they can't do it here, in this project. And he say if they just move someplace else and do it, what's the point of moving them out, and I say the point is, I said I would. And he sit there awhile, and then he say, 'I can dig it.' And he sit awhile longer and he say, 'But I can't let you and the Mickey chase me out, you understand. I can't let you dis me.' And I say, 'You willing to die for that?' And he say, 'What else I got?' "

We were all quiet. The waiter came silently by and poured champagne into our glasses and returned the bottle to the ice bucket. It was a quiet room. The tables were spaced so that everyone had space around them. The conversation was muted. There was thick carpeting on the floors so that the waiters in tuxedos moved as silently as assassins among the patrons, their shirtfronts gleaming in the soft light.

"I can dig it," I said.

129

26

Belson called me at 6:30 in the morning while I was making coffee.

"Piece you gave us doesn't check out," he said.

"It didn't kill the kid and her baby?"

"No."

"Got a next of kin?" I said.

"No. Only way we ID'd her was that the kid was born at Boston City and they had a footprint."

"Where'd she live?" I said.

"No address."

"Baby's father?"

"Don't know."

"Hot on the trail," I said.

"You bet."

"Well, she had to live somewhere."

"Yeah."

"And there had to be a father."

"Yeah."

"So I guess I'll have to find him."

"Sure," Belson said and hung up the phone.

Susan was at the kitchen counter eating some kind of bran cereal with orange segments on it and drinking hot water with a wedge of lemon. Pearl sat on the floor, watching closely.

"The gun you took from the gang kids?"

"Yeah." I put some cream in my coffee and two sugars. Susan was ready for the day. She had on a gray suit, and her thick black hair gleamed with ogalala nut oil or whatever she had washed it with.

"Full day?" I said.

She put her empty cereal bowl down for Pearl.

"Patients all morning, and then I have my seminar at Tuft," she said.

She stood up. I looked at her. I felt the same feeling I always felt when I looked at her. It was almost a way to monitor my existence. Like a pulse. If I looked at her and didn't feel the feeling, I'd know I had died.

"Be home for supper?" she said.

"Depends," I said. "If I find the guy who killed the kid and her baby, and Hawk and I get Double Deuce stabilized, I may be home by midafternoon."

She leaned forward and kissed me. I patted her on the butt.

"You'll not take it as a gesture of no-confidence should I go ahead and eat without you?" she said.

"You shrinks are a cynical lot," I said.

Susan went downstairs to see patients. Pearl went to the door with her and then came back to supervise my breakfast. I was having a turkey cutlet sandwich on an onion roll with a lot of Heinz 57 sauce on it. I gave Pearl a bite.

"Hell of an improvement over bran and orange segments," I said.

Pearl was too loyal to comment but I knew she agreed.

27

I picked Erin Macklin up on Cardinal Road in front of the Garvey School. It was raining as she came down the stairs, and she was wearing a short green slicker over tan slacks. On her feet were low-cut L. L. Bean gum rubber boots with leather tops. She was bareheaded. She looked like somebody's suburban housewife on her way to a Little League hockey game. The fact that she didn't seem to be worried that her hair was getting wet, however, proved that she wasn't somebody's suburban housewife at all.

"Your friend is sitting alone at Double Deuce?" she said when she got in the car.

"He seems calm about it," I said.

"Ah yes," she said, "the ironist."

"You know me that well on such brief notice?" I said.

"Your reputation precedes you," she said. "It is coloring my judgment."

Cardinal Road was once Irish. White Catholic people my age had been born there. The houses were nearly all clapboard three-deckers with flat roofs and bay windows and a piazza across the back at each level. The doors were generally to the left side. There was a small porch, three steps to a walk made of cement, and a tiny yard. Along Cardinal Road the yards were neat and mostly enclosed with a low-clipped barberry hedge. On the minuscule lawns, greening in the spring rain, there were tricycles and big wheels. The houses were painted. In the windows there were curtains. It looked like most of the other blue-collar neighborhoods in Boston. But in this one, every face was black.

"I need more help," I said.

Erin's eyes moved carefully over the cityscape as we drove.

"Tell me what you need," she said.

"A young girl, not quite fifteen, was murdered," I said. "Around Double Deuce. She had her three-month-old baby with her. The baby was killed too."

"Boy or girl?" Erin said.

"Girl. Crystal. You're right. She shouldn't be anonymous."

"Yes," Erin said. "Helps to focus."

"Girl's name was Devona Jefferson," I said.

"I don't know her."

"Nobody seems to, but somebody did. I want to find somebody who knew her."

"Why?"

"Because I want to know who killed her."

"And when you know?" Erin said.

"Depends. If there's evidence we'll give it to the cops."

"If there isn't?"

"We'll see," I said.

"Would you take some sort of action yourself?"

"I might."

"And your friend?"

"He might."

We turned onto Alewife Way. It had the same three-deckers, the same tiny yards. But the yards had no grass, and the rain had made the bare earth muddy. The houses seemed to have sagged more on Alewife, and the front porches had sagged. There was a sway in the piazzas. The houses badly needed painting. Many of the windows were patched with cardboard, and the yards were littered. There were empty bottles of Wild Irish Rose, and the plastic rings that six-packs came in, small brown paper sacks, and fast-food wrappers, some empty wine cooler cartons, and empty cigarette hard-packs with the tops open. People were out in the rain, but they seemed to hate it and walked in sullen slouches, hunching close to walls and standing in the doorway of the variety store with the thick wire mesh over the windows.

At the corner of Colonial Drive was a playground: some blacktop inside a chain-link fence with two metal back-

135

boards. One rim had no net, the other had one made of wire mesh.

"Bury one from the corner," I said, "and it won't swish, it'll clang."

"Mesh nets are supposed to last longer. But they don't. The kids use them for weapons."

I nodded. "Gather one end and tape it," I said. "Kids make do, don't they."

"Yes," she said. "They are often quite ingenious. They function barely at all in school, and the standard aptitude tests seem beyond them, and yet they are very intelligent about surviving in fearful conditions. They are often resourceful, they fashion what they need out of what they have. They endure in conditions that would simply suffocate most of the Harvard senior class."

"Probably more than one kind of intelligence," I said.

"Probably," Erin said. "Let's talk to these kids."

There were six of them leaning against the chain-link fence in the rain. One of them had a basketball. All of them wore Adidas hightops and stone-washed jeans, and purple Lakers jackets. Three of them had white Laker hats, two wore them backwards. They seemed at ease standing in the rain. The one with the basketball was dribbling it around himself behind his back through his legs in a figure-eight pattern. The others were smoking. Their faces froze into the uniform look of tough indifference when I pulled up. They thought we were cops. When Erin got out they relaxed, though the look flickered on again when they saw me.

"Quintin," she said. "How are you?"

She put her hand out and the boy with the ball tucked it under his left arm and slapped her right palm once, gently.

"Lady Beige," he said. "Looking good."

He didn't look at me.

"He's not a cop," Erin said. "He's with me."

Quintin shrugged. The tough look flickered again. They would never be easy with a big white guy in their yard, and the look, if it wasn't quite tough hostile, wasn't welcoming.

"Girl named Devona Jefferson was killed a little while ago over in front of Double Deuce. She had a baby. Baby's name was Crystal. They killed her too."

Quintin shrugged again.

"Do you know her?"

"What her name?"

"Devona," Erin said. "Devona Jefferson."

"Ain't down with the Silks," Quintin said. "What they shoot her with?"

"A nine millimeter," I said.

"Use a fresh pipe anyway," Quintin said.

"You don't know her?" I said.

"Hell, no," Quintin said. "Anybody know her?"

The other five all said no they didn't know her. Erin said thank you and we got back in the car. We drove around in the rain talking with people for the rest of the day, not finding anything out.

28

It was still raining the next morning when I checked in with Hawk at Double Deuce. There was no sign of life in the project. The rain made Hawk's dark green Jaguar look black as it beaded and slid off the finish. I parked next to him and got out and got in his car. Jackie was sitting in the front seat with him.

"We been renewed?" I said.

She smiled.

"Marge has forgiven you."

"Thank God," I said. "She finds me irresistible?"

"We'd already hyped the thing too much informally. We

didn't want some columnist to question why we'd said we were going to do this feature and then backed off."

"Almost like finding you irresistible," Hawk said. "How 'bout the detection?"

"I'm seeing a lot of the ghetto."

Hawk nodded.

"Nobody has confessed," I said.

"Only a matter of time," Hawk said. "Nothing folks in the ghetto want to do more than to find some big honkie and confess to him. Been wanting to myself."

"I don't want to hear it," I said. "It would take too long."

"What are you detecting?" Jackie said.

"Who killed Devona and Crystal Jefferson."

"Really?"

"Un huh."

"Well, I mean I knew that was part of what you, we're, ah, supposed to do. But, I mean what about the police?"

"Police have hung it up," I said.

"And what about here?"

"You and Hawk have that covered," I said.

"And we got Marge Eagen," Hawk said, "for backup."

"Can you move around in the black community?"

"I have a guide," I said.

"And you think you can do what the police have given up on?"

"You bet," I said.

"I don't want to sound either naive or cynical, I don't know which," Jackie said, "but why?"

"Why do I think I can find him?"

139

"No, why are you willing to try?"

"Somebody ought to," I said.

Jackie stared at me. The rain came down on the car roof in its pleasant way. The sound of rain on a car roof always made me feel comfortable.

"That's it?" Jackie said.

"Yeah."

"Why should somebody *ought to?*"

"Fourteen-year-old kid got murdered, and a three-month-old kid got murdered, and as far as anyone can see they had nothing to do with it. That shouldn't go unremarked."

"I'll be damned," Jackie said.

CHAPTER

29

It was nearly noon when Erin and I pulled into a fast-food hamburger place on Lister Way. Three kids were sitting in a gray and black Aerostar van with the doors open and the tape deck blaring. The parking lot was crowded and the restaurant was full of people getting out of the rain. Nobody was over twenty.

"This time let's try you stay in the car," Erin said.

"Okay."

I sat while she got out and went to the van. Again she put out her hand, again the gentle slap. Then she got in the backseat of the van and I couldn't see her. The two kids in front turned to talk with her. The rain made the bright

141

colors of the pseudocolonial restaurant shiny and clean looking. There was a litter of hamburger cartons and paper wrappers and cardboard cups among the cars, and the trash barrel near the front door of the place was overfilled. With Erin out of sight I was the only white face in a sea of black ones. If I weren't so self-assured it would have made me a little uncomfortable. If I had been uncomfortable no one would have noticed. No one paid any attention to me at all.

I shut the motor off. The rain collected on the windshield and made the colors of the restaurant streak into a kind of impressionist blur. *Here's looking at you, Claude Monet.* The restaurant and its parking lot stood alone, the only principle of order in a panorama of urban blight. There were vacant lots on both sides of the place. Each one littered with the detritus of buildings long since dismantled. Across the street was a salvage yard with spiraling coils of razor wire atop a chain-link fence. Even prettified by the rain this was not the garden at Givenchy.

Erin got back in the car. "Want a cheeseburger?" she said.

"Too far from medical help," I said.

Erin smiled and closed the car door.

"These kids know Devona Jefferson," she said.

"And?"

"She had a boyfriend named Tallboy."

"In a gang?"

"They're all in gangs," Erin said. "It's how they survive."

"Know which gang?"

"Yes," Erin said. "Tallboy's a member of the Dillard Street Posse."

"Progress," I said.

"More than that," Erin said. "I know him."

CHAPTER

30

Tallboy wasn't anywhere we looked for the rest of the day. Erin and I stopped in my office for a drink.

"Some of them are only seven or eight years old," Erin said.

She had half a glass of Irish whiskey which she held in both hands.

"Some of the older gang kids will recruit the wannabes to carry the weapon, or the drugs, even sometimes do the shooting—they're juveniles. If they're caught, the penalty is lighter. And the little ones are thrilled. Peer acceptance, peer approval." She smiled a little and sipped her whiskey. "Upward mobility," she said.

I nodded. Outside the window the rain was still with us, straight down in the windless darkness, making the pleasant hush hush sound it makes.

"The thing is," I said, "is that that's true. The gangs are upward mobility."

"Oh, certainly," Erin said. It was obviously so ordinary a part of what she knew that she hadn't thought that anyone might not know it. "These kids are capitalists. They watch television and they believe it. They have the values they've seen on the tube. They think that the Cosby family is reality, and it is so remote from their reality that they find their own life unbearable. The inequity enrages them. It is not arrogance that causes so many explosions of violence, it's the opposite."

"Would the term 'low self-esteem' be useful?" I said.

"Accurate," Erin said. "But not very useful. None of the things people say on talk shows are very useful. What they see on television is a life entirely different than theirs, and as far as they can see, what makes the difference is money. The way for them to get money is to sell drugs or to steal from people who sell drugs—there isn't anybody else in their world that has money to steal—and since either enterprise is dangerous, the gang offers protection, identity, even a kind of nurturance."

"Everybody needs some," I said.

The whiskey was nearly vaporous when I sipped it, less liquid than a kind of warm miasma in the mouth. It was warm in my office, and dry, and in the quiet light the two of us were comfortable.

"Where do you get yours?" I said.

"Nurturance?" She sipped her whiskey again, bending toward the glass a little as she drank. Then she raised her head and smiled at me. "From the kids, I suppose. I guess the gangs provide me meaning and belonging and emotional sustenance."

"Whatever works," I said.

We were quiet briefly while the rain fell and the whiskey worked. There was no uneasiness in the silence. Either of us would talk when we had something to say. Neither of us felt the need to talk when we didn't.

"Do you know Maslow's hierarchy of needs?" Erin said.

"Don't even know Maslow," I said.

"Maslow's studies indicate that humans have a descending order of fundamental needs: physical fulfillment, food, warmth, that sort of thing; then safety, love, and belonging; and self-esteem. Whoever—or whatever—provides for those needs will command loyalty and love."

"Which the gangs do."

"Yes," Erin said. "They do."

Again we were quiet. Erin finished her whiskey and held her glass out. I poured her another drink. Me too.

"There's even a girls' gang," Erin said. "Really vicious, hostile."

"I will make no remark about the female of the species," I said.

"Ghetto life is sexist in the extreme," Erin said. "Among the gangs, women are second-class citizens. Good for sex and little else. Maybe it has to do with a matriarchal society. Maybe all sexism does—the struggle between son and mother over son's freedom. I have no theories on it—I have no theories on anything. I haven't time."

She drank again and seemed lost for a moment in thoughts I had no access to.

"You were talking about a female gang," I said.

Erin shook her head, half smiling. "The Crockettes. More macho than anyone. One of the girls, name was Whistle, I don't know why, stabbed her mother and put out a contract on her stepfather."

"And then demanded leniency because she was an orphan."

"It is almost like a joke, isn't it?" Erin said. "She paid off the contract with sex. Even in the toughest of female gangs, that's their edge, they pay for what they want by fucking."

Erin's voice was hard. I knew she'd chosen the word carefully.

"So finally, no matter what else they do, they perpetuate their status," I said.

Erin nodded slowly, gazing past me at the dark vertical rain.

"The only thing that can save them, boys or girls, the only thing that works," she said, "is if they can get some sort of positive relationship with an adult. They have no role models, nobody to demonstrate a way of life better than the one they're in . . . or the church. I know it sounds silly, but if these kids get religion, they have something. The Muslims have saved a lot."

"Another kind of gang."

147

"Sure—Muslims, Baptists, the Marine Corps. Anybody, anything that can provide for Maslow's hierarchy, that can show them that they are part of something, that they matter."

She was leaning forward in her chair, the whiskey held in two hands in her lap and forgotten. I raised my glass toward her and gestured and took a drink.

"What I hope for you, Sister Macklin, is that you never lose this . . . but you get something else too."

She smiled at me.

"That would be nice," she said.

31

I got home just after Susan's last patient had departed. Susan was on the phone. Which she was a lot. She knew more people than Ivana Trump, and she talked to all of them, nearly every day, after work. Pearl was eating some dry dog food mixed with water in the kitchen and was profoundly ambivalent whether to greet me or keep eating. She made one fast dash at me and then returned to her supper. But she wagged her tail vigorously as she ate. Good enough. Susan waved at me but stayed on the phone. I didn't mind. I liked listening to her talk on the phone. It was a performance—animated, intimate, compelling, rich with overtones, radiant with interest. I didn't even know to whom she was talking, or about what. I just liked the sound of it, the way I like the sound of music.

I got a pork tenderloin out and brushed it with honey and sprinkled it with rosemary and put it in the oven. While it roasted I mixed up some corn flour biscuits and let them sit while I tossed a salad of white beans and peppers and doused it with some olive oil and cilantro. When the pork was done I took it out and let it rest while I baked the biscuits. I put some boysenberry jam out to have with the biscuits and sat down to eat.

I had already put away a biscuit when Susan hung up the phone and walked across the kitchen and gave me a kiss. She pursed her lips slightly and then nodded.

"Boysenberry," she said.

"Yes," I said.

"We got it last fall at that stand in Belfast, Maine."

"Sensitive palate and good memory," I said.

"And great kisser?"

"Everyone says so," I said. "You want a little supper?"

She smiled and shook her head.

"I'll have something later," she said. "I still have to go to the club."

"Aerobics?"

"Yes. I'm taking a step class and then I'll probably do some weights. You eat much too early for me."

I nodded.

"Any progress today?" Susan said.

"Some," I said. "We got the name of Devona's boy-friend."

"Can you find him?" Susan said.

"He can run," I said. "But he can't hide."

"Isn't that a sports saying of some sort?"

"Yeah. Joe Louis said it about Billy Conn."

"Do you think he had to do with killing her?"

"We find him," I said, "we'll ask."

Susan nodded. She looked at my supper. "That looks good," she said. "Well, I've got to get moving. I still have my revolting workout."

"I know this is silly," I said, "but if you find it revolting, why do you do it?"

"That's silly," Susan said.

"I knew it was when I said it. Well, it's working great, anyway."

"Thank you," she said and hurried off to change.

As I ate my supper with the first round of the playoffs on the tube, I thought about how I had almost never seen Susan when she wasn't in a hurry. I didn't mind it exactly, but I had noticed it less when we lived apart.

CHAPTER

32

We were on Hafford Avenue, with the enduring rain coming steadily against the windshield and the wipers barely
holding their own.

"I thought posses were Jamaican," I said.

"Language changes very fast here. Now it just means a
small gang. There are gangs with five or six kids in them if
that's all there are in the neighborhood," Erin said.

We turned onto McCrory Street, a block from Double
Deuce, and left onto Dillard Street and pulled up into the
apron of an abandoned gas station. The pumps were gone,
and the place where they had been torn out of the island
looked like an open wound. The station windows had been

replaced with plywood; and the plywood, and the walls of the station itself, were covered completely with fluorescent graffiti. The overhead door to the service bay was up and half a dozen kids sat in the bay on recycled furniture and looked at the rain. There was a thunderous rap group on at peak volume, and the kids were passing around a jug of white Concord grape wine.

"The one with the wispy goatee is Tallboy," Erin said.

He was sprawled on a broken chaise lounge: plumpish, and not very tall, wearing a red sweatshirt with the hood up.

"Tallboy?" I said.

"He usually drinks beer in the twenty-four-ounce cans," Erin said. She rolled down the window and called to him.

"Tallboy, I need to talk with you."

"Who you with, Miss Macklin?" Tallboy said.

He hadn't moved but he'd tightened up. All of them had, and they gazed out at me in dark silence from their cave.

"A friend," she said. "I need to talk. Can you come sit in the car?"

Tallboy got up slowly and came even more slowly toward the car. He walked with a kind of wide-legged swagger. He might have been a little drunk. When he was in the back he left the door open.

"What you need, Miss Macklin?"

"You knew Devona Jefferson," she said.

"Yeah?"

"I know you did, Tallboy. She was your girlfriend."

"So?"

153

"And she was killed."

"Don't know nothing about that," he said. He looked hard at me. "Who you?" he said.

"Guy looking for the people killed your girlfriend."

"You DT?"

"No."

"So what you care who piped Devona?"

"They killed your baby, too," I said.

"Hey, man, what you talking shit to me for? You don't even know that my little girl."

I waited. Tallboy glanced back toward the open garage where the jug was.

"She prob'ly was," he said. "She look like me."

He looked back toward the wine again. I reached under the front seat and brought out a bottle of Glenfiddich Single Malt Scotch Whiskey. It's handy to have around, because there are times when it is a better bribe than money.

"Try a little of this," I said.

Tallboy stared at it and then took the bottle and swallowed some.

"Damn," he said, "that is some juke, man. That is some bad beverage."

"You know who killed her?" I said.

His eyes slid away from mine and he took another pull on the Glenfiddich. Then he looked back at me and his eyes were tearing. He was drunker than I thought and the scotch was moving him along.

"Sure you do. But you don't care. You want them to get away with it."

154

He shifted his gaze to Erin.

"That ain't so, Miss Macklin."

"I know," she said. "I know you don't want them to get away with it." She put her hand over the back of the seat and he took it and she held his hand. The tears were running down his face now. I was quiet. We waited. He drank again.

"Nine my fucking baby," he said. "Motherfuckers."

"Who?" Erin said.

"Motherfucking Hobarts." He was mumbling. I had to listen hard. "Dealing some classic for them and I a little short, I gonna pay them. I just a little short that minute. And motherfuckers nine my little girl."

"You sure?" I said.

"Who else it gonna be?" Tallboy said.

"You know which Hobart?" I said.

He shook his head.

"It ain't over," he said. "We gon take care of business. Can't fuck with us and ride." His head had sunk to his chest. He was talking into the bottle . . . and out of it. "Can't dis a Dillard and ride, man."

I looked at Erin and gestured with my head.

"Thank you, Tallboy," she said. "You know how to call me up, don't you?"

Tallboy nodded.

"If you want to talk about this any more, you call me," she said.

"Yass, Miss Macklin."

Tallboy lurched out of the car holding the bottle of Glen-

155

fiddich. He held it up in one hand and waved it at the rest of the posse.

"Fine," he said and started to say something else, and didn't seem able to and lurched on into the garage, out of the rain.

I slid the car into gear and pulled away.

"He isn't even tough," I said.

"Of course he isn't," Erin said. "He tries, but he's not."

"Tough is the only way to survive in here," I said.

"I know," Erin said. "Some of them are tougher than one would think possible . . . and some of them aren't."

33

Erin and Hawk and I were nibbling at some Irish whiskey in my office. It was dark in the Back Bay. The rain had stopped, but everything was still wet and the streets gleamed blackly when I looked out the window.

"Say the Hobarts did it is saying Major did it," Hawk said.

"If Tallboy's right," I said.

"Tallboy will never testify," Erin said.

"No need," Hawk said.

"Spenser said something like that," Erin said. "I asked him if he might take action of his own. He said he might."

Hawk smiled. He drank some whiskey. And rolled it a

little on his tongue and swallowed. Then he stood and went to the sink in the corner and added a little tap water. He stood while he sampled it, nodded to himself, and came back to his chair.

Erin said, "What would you consider appropriate action?"

"We could kill him," Hawk said.

Erin looked at me.

"You?" she said.

"Somebody is going to," I said.

"I don't think you would," she said, "simply execute him yourself."

I let that slide. There was nothing there for me.

She looked back at Hawk.

"You feel no sympathy for these kids, do you," she said.

Hawk looked friendly but puzzled.

"Got nothing to do with sympathy," Hawk said. "Got to do with work. Work I do you kill people sometimes. Major seems as good a person to kill as anybody."

"When you were twenty," Erin said, "you probably weren't so different from Major."

"Am now," Hawk said. He drank another swallow of whiskey.

Erin was holding her whiskey glass in both hands. She stared into it quietly for a moment.

"You got out," she said. "You were no better off than Major, probably, and you got out."

Hawk looked at her pleasantly.

"Now you are a free man," Erin said. "Autonomous, sure of yourself, unashamed, unafraid. Nobody's nigger."

Hawk listened politely. He seemed interested.

"And you've paid a terrible price," she said.

"Worth the cost," Hawk said.

"I know what you're like," she said. "I see young men who, were they stronger, or braver, or smarter, would grow up to be like you. Young men who have put away feelings. Who make a kind of Thoreauvian virtue out of stripping their emotional lives to the necessities."

"Probably seem a good idea at the time," Hawk said.

"Of course it does," Erin said. "It is probably what they must do to live. But what a tragedy, to put aside, in order to live, the things that make it worth anything to live."

"Worse," Hawk said, "if you do that and don't live anyway."

"Yes," Erin said.

We all sat for a while nursing the whiskey, listening to the damp traffic sounds from Berkeley Street, where it crosses Boylston. Erin was still staring down into her glass. When she raised her head, I could see that her eyes were moist.

"It's not just Major that you mourn for," I said.

She shook her head silently.

"If Hawk talked about things like this, which he doesn't, he might say that you misread him. That what you see as the absence of emotion is something rather more like calm."

"Calm?"

I nodded.

"I worse than Major," Hawk said quietly. "And I got better, and I got out, and I got out by myself."

"And that makes you calm?"

"I know I can trust me," Hawk said.

"And you'd kill Major?"

"Don't know if I will, know I could."

"And you wouldn't mind," Erin said. "I can't understand that."

Erin's glance rested on Hawk. She wasn't staring at her whiskey now.

"I can't understand that."

"I know," Hawk said.

"I don't want to understand that," Erin said.

"I know that too," Hawk said.

34

The rain had paused, but it was still overcast, and cold for spring, when Hawk pulled his Jaguar into the quadrangle in front of Double Deuce. He stopped. In front of us, on the wet blacktop where we normally parked, was a body. Hawk let the car idle while we got out and looked. It was Tallboy, lying on his back, his mouth ajar, his eyes staring up at the rainclouds, one leg doubled under the other. No need to feel for a pulse, he was stiff with death. Hawk and I both knew it.

"Know him?" Hawk said.

"Name was Tallboy," I said. "He was Devona Jefferson's boyfriend and maybe the baby's father."

"You just talked to him."

"Yeah."

"So he here for us."

"Yeah."

Hawk nodded. He looked slowly around the project. Nothing moved. He looked back down at Tallboy.

"Don't seem too tall," he said.

"He liked the big beer cans," I said.

Hawk nodded some more, still looking almost absently at the boy's body. His clothes were wet, which meant he'd been left here while it was still raining. There was a dark patch of blood on the front of his sweatshirt, in the middle of his chest.

"Ain't no trash can fire," Hawk said.

He was surveying the project again.

"He told me he was going to even up for his girlfriend," I said. "He was drunk."

"Probably drunk when he tried," Hawk said, his eyes moving carefully over the silent buildings.

"Figure they're watching from somewhere?" I said.

"They kids," Hawk said. "They got to be watching, see what we do."

I was still looking at Tallboy. I didn't bother looking for the gang. If they were there, Hawk would see them. Tallboy appeared to be maybe sixteen in death's frozen repose. Soft faced, not mean. Kind of kid would probably really rather have stayed home and talked with his mother and his aunts, if he'd had any, and they were sober, and their boyfriends wouldn't slap him around. Might have not gotten killed if I hadn't gone and talked with him and gotten him stirred up about who killed his girlfriend and her baby, that might have been his baby. He probably liked the baby, not like a father; not to change diapers, and earn money, and take care of—that would have been beyond him. But she'd have been fun to hug, and she'd have been cute, and he would probably have liked it when the three of them were alone and they could play together. It had started to rain again, not much, a light drizzle that beaded sparsely on his upturned defenseless face.

Hawk said, "Third building from the right, second floor, three middle windows."

I glanced up slowly, and not toward the windows. I glanced obliquely past them and looked out of the corner of my eye. There was a shade half drawn and some movement behind it.

"What makes you think it's them?" I said.

"Been here every day," Hawk said. "While you and the schoolteacher dashing around the ghetto. Nobody live on that floor."

"Well, maybe some evasive action and come up behind them?" I said.

"Sure," Hawk said. "Little acting, too." He gestured suddenly at the vacant lot across the street, I whirled to look where he pointed.

"Now we hustle into the car," Hawk said.

And we did, and pulled out of the quadrangle with Hawk's tires screaming as they spun on the wet pavement. We went around the corner onto McCrory Street and

163

slammed into the alley back of the third building. Hawk popped the trunk and we each grabbed a shotgun. As we moved toward the back door of the building each of us pumped a shell into the chamber at the same moment.

"We could set this to music," I said.

The back entryway had been padlocked, but the hasp had been jimmied loose and it hung, with its still intact padlock attached, limply beside the partly open door. We went in, I to the right, Hawk to the left. We were in a dim cellar. It was full of cardboard boxes which had gotten wet and collapsed, spilling whatever had once been in them onto the floor, where whatever soaked the boxes had, over time, reduced it to an indeterminate mass of mildewing stuff. In the middle of the cellar was a defunct boiler with rust staining the sides of it and adding to the indiscernible detritus on the floor.

We moved past the boiler to the stairs. Hawk, in hightop Reebok pump-ups, moved through the trash beneath the building like a dark ghost, holding the eight-pound shotgun in his right hand as if it were a wand. It was as if he were floating. We went up the two flights of stairs without a sound. In the dim, claustrophobic corridor we paused, Hawk counting the doors until he found what we wanted. He stepped to it and put his ear against it and listened. There was litter nearly ankle deep in places all up and down the corridor—broken glass, fast-food paper and plastic, beer cans, and food scraps that were no longer identifiable. In the silence while Hawk listened I could hear vermin rustle in the trash. I waited. Hawk listened. Then he smiled at me and nodded.

With the shotgun in my right hand I reached over with my left and took hold of the knob and turned it slowly. It gave and the door opened inward and Hawk went in and left. I came in behind him and moved right. There were eight kids in there grouped near the windows, wondering where we were. Beside the window was a large cable spool, standing on end. On top of it lay a Tec-9 automatic which would fire thirty-two rounds if we let it.

One kid spun toward the gun. It was the same small, quick one I'd taken the Browning from in the van. I fired at the cable spool and hit it, chips of plastic flew off the handle of the Tec-9, and a ragged chunk of the wooden top flew up as well. The handgun ricocheted off the wall and bounced on the floor, the clip separated and skittered across the room, some of the shotgun pellets pocked the wall beyond.

Everyone froze.

In the reverberating silence after the gunshot, Hawk's voice was almost piercing.

"Where's Major?" Hawk said quietly.

No one said anything.

"Guess he won't be going down for it," Hawk said.

No one said a word. All eight stood in perfect stillness. Under the gun like that they didn't seem frightful. They seemed like scared kids whose prank had gotten out of hand. They were that, but they were the other thing too, they were kids who would shoot a fourteen-year-old girl

165

and her three-month-old baby. They were kids who would gun down her boyfriend and leave him as a statement. That was the hard part, remembering that they weren't inhuman predators, and that they were. *One must have a mind of winter,* I thought, *to behold the nothing that is not there and the nothing that is.*

"Any of you guys read Wallace Stevens?" I said.

No one spoke. The shotgun felt solid and weighty as I held it. The faint smell of the exploded shell lingered.

"We'll check the slug that killed Tallboy," Hawk said. "And we'll check the Tec-9, and we'll see whose prints are on it."

Hawk let his gaze rest quietly on the kid who'd first made a move for the gun.

"You the shooter, Shoe?"

Hawk was making it up as he went along. It wasn't clear to me that the Tec-9 would fire even a test round anymore, and it probably had more prints on it than a subway door, but Shoe seemed impressed.

"I didn't trace nobody," he said.

"You think you won't go down for it?" Hawk said. "You think maybe you gotta lot of influence downtown, and they won't drop you in a jar as soon as we bring you in? If we feel like bringing you in?"

"I didn't trace Tallboy," Shoe said.

"Don't matter if you did or didn't," Hawk said. "We prove you did and it's one less problem for Double Deuce. Fact we prove you all accessories and we got Double Deuce's problems solved."

"We didn't do nothing." It was a fat kid they called Goodyear. His voice had an asthmatic whisper around the edges of it. "We just looking out the window, see what's happening."

"We got you at the scene of a crime, with the murder weapon," I said. "There's three unsolved murders cleaned up if we can tag you with them. You think we can't?"

"Shoe didn't do it," Goodyear said.

"Yeah, he did," Hawk said.

"No," Shoe said. His voice had outrage in it. The other kids muttered that he really hadn't.

"He didn't," Goodyear said.

"Move out," Hawk said. "We'll call downtown from my car."

Nobody moved. Still holding the shotgun in one hand, Hawk put the muzzle against Shoe's upper lip, right under his nose.

"Going down anyway, Shoe, may as well die here as Walpole."

"They don't burn nobody in this state," Shoe said.

"For killing a three-month-old baby?" Hawk smiled.

"I never done that," Shoe said.

"And her momma."

"No," Shoe said, his head tipped back a little by the pressure of the shotgun muzzle.

"And Tallboy. You be lucky to make it to Walpole."

"No," Shoe said.

"Course it coulda been Major," he said.

"No. Major didn't," Shoe said.

167

Hawk was silent for a long time while we all stood there and waited. Finally he lowered the shotgun.

"Beat it," he said. They all stood motionless for a moment, then Shoe walked past him and out the open door. One by one they followed. No one spoke. In a moment it was just Hawk and me alone in the dingy room with the damaged remnants of a Tec-9.

35

"Isn't that fascinating," Susan said. "They wouldn't budge."

We were sitting at the counter in the kitchen. I was drinking some Catamount beer, and Susan, to be sociable, was occasionally wetting her bottom lip in a glass of Cabernet Blanc. Pearl sprawled on the floor, her four feet out straight, her eyes nearly closed, occasionally glancing over to make sure no food had made a surreptitious appearance.

"They were scared," I said. "Hawk could scare Mount Rushmore. But they wouldn't give in."

"It's interesting, isn't it. These kids have many of the same virtues and vices that other kids have, misapplied."

"They're applied to what's there," I said.

Susan nodded. "And the consequences may be fatal," she said.

Across the counter, in the small kitchen, there was evidence that Susan had prepared a meal . . . or that the kitchen had been ransacked. Since there was a pot of something simmering on the stove, I assumed the former.

"The thing is," I said, "we all knew Major did the killing. They knew it; we knew it; they knew we knew it; we knew they knew—"

"You admire their loyalty," Susan said.

She was wearing black spandex tights and a leotard top. The outfit revealed nearly everything about her body. I looked at her eyes, and felt as I always did, that I could breathe more deeply when I looked at her, that the air was oxygen rich, and that we would live forever.

"Windows of the soul," I said.

She grinned at me.

"Augmented with just a touch of eye liner," she said.

"What's in the pot?" I said.

She glanced back at the stove.

"Jesus," she said and jumped up and dashed around the counter. She picked up a big spoon and jostled the pot lid off with it. She looked in and smiled.

"It's okay," she said.

"Maybe Christmas," I said, "I'll buy you a potholder."

"I've got some, but I couldn't find it right away and I was afraid it would burn."

She was trying to balance the pot lid on her big spoon

170

and put it back on the pot. It teetered, she touched it with her left hand to balance it, and burned her hand, and flinched and the lid fell to the floor.

"Fuck," she said.

Pearl had leapt to attention when the lid hit the floor and now was sitting behind the legs of my stool and looking out at Susan with something that might have been disapproval. Susan saw her.

"Everyone's a goddamned critic," she said.

"What is it?" I said neutrally.

"Brunswick stew," Susan said. "There was a recipe in the paper."

She found one potholder under an overturned colander and used it to pick up the pot lid and put it back on the pot.

"One of my favorites," I said.

"I know," Susan said. "It's why I made it."

"I'll like it," I said.

"And if you don't," she said, "lie."

"It is my every intention," I said.

She set the counter in front of us, got me another beer, and ladled two servings of Brunswick stew into our plates. I took a bite. It was pretty good. I had some more.

"Do I detect a dumpling in here?" I said.

"No," Susan said. "I tried to thicken the gravy. What you detect is some flour in a congealed glump."

"What you do," I said, "is mix the flour in a little cold water first, then when the slurry is smooth you stir it into the stew."

"Gee, isn't that smart," Susan said.

171

I knew she didn't mean it. I decided not to make other helpful suggestions. We ate quietly for a while. The congealed flour lumps had tasted better when I thought they were dumplings. When I finished I got up and walked around Pearl to the stove and got a second helping.

"Oh, for Christ sake don't patronize me," Susan said.

"I'm hungry," I said. "The stew's good. Are we saving it for breakfast?"

"The stew's not good. You're just eating it to make me feel good."

"Not true, but if it were, why would that be so bad?"

"Oh, shit," Susan said, and her eyes began to fill.

I said, "Suze, you never cry."

"It's not working," she said. Her voice was very tight and very shaky. She got up and left the kitchen and went in the bedroom and closed the door.

I stood for a while holding the stew and looking after her. Then I looked at Pearl. She was focused on the plate of stew.

"The thing is," I said to Pearl, "she's right."

And I put the plate down for Pearl to finish.

36

Tony Marcus agreed to meet us at a muffin shop on the arcade in South Station.

"Tony like muffins?" I said.

"Tony likes open public places," Hawk said.

"Makes sense," I said. "Get trapped in a place like Locke-Ober, you could get umbrella'd to death."

South Station was new, almost. They'd jacked up the old façade and slid a new station in behind it. Where once pigeons had flown about in the semidarkness, and winos had slept fragrantly on the benches, there were now muffin shops and lots of light and a model train set. What had once been the dank remnant of the old railroad days was now as slick and cheery as the food circus in a shopping mall.

The muffin shop was there, to the right, past the frozen lo-fat yogurt stand. Tony Marcus was there at a cute little iron filigree table, alone. At the next table was his bodyguard, a stolid black man about the size of Nairobi. The bodyguard's name was Billy. Tony was a middle-sized black guy, a little soft, with a careful moustache. I always thought he looked like Billy Eckstine, but Hawk never saw it. We stopped at the counter. I bought two coffees, gave one to Hawk, and went to Tony's table.

Tony nodded very slightly when we arrived. Billy looked at us as if we were dust motes. Billy's eyes were very small. He looked like a Cape buffalo. I shot at him with a forefinger and thumb.

"Hey, Billy," I said. "Every time I see you you get more winsome."

Billy gazed at me without expression.

Tony said, "You want a muffin?"

Hawk and I both shook our heads.

"Good muffins," Tony said. "Praline chocolate chip are excellent."

Hawk said, "Jesus Christ."

Tony had two on a paper plate in front of him. He picked one up and took a bite out of it, the way you'd eat an apple.

"So what you need?" he said around the mouthful of muffin.

"Gang of kids running drugs out of a housing project at Twenty-two Hobart Street," I said.

Tony nodded and chewed on his muffin.

"Couple people been killed," I said.

Tony shook his head. "Fucking younger generation," he said.

"Going to hell in a handbasket," I said. "Tenants at Double Deuce hired Hawk and me to bring order out of chaos there."

Marcus looked at his bodyguard. "You hear how he talks, Billy? 'Order out of chaos.' Ain't that something?"

"And the most successful local television show in the country is doing a five-part investigative series on the whole deal."

It got Tony's attention.

"What television show?"

"*Marge Eagen, Live,*" I said.

"The blonde broad with the big tits?"

I smiled. Hawk smiled.

"What do you mean, an investigation?" Tony said.

"What's wrong in the ghetto," Hawk said. "Who's selling drugs, how to save kids from the gangs, how to make black folks just like white folks."

Marcus was silent for the time it took him to eat the rest of his second muffin.

When he finished he said, "You in on that?"

"Sorta parallel," I said.

Tony pursed his lips slightly and nodded, and kept nodding, as if he'd forgotten he was doing it. He picked up his coffee cup and discovered it was empty. Billy got him another one. Tony stirred three spoonfuls of sugar carefully into the coffee and laid his spoon down and took a sip. Then he looked at me.

"So?" he said.

"The investigation is centered on the project," I said. "And"—I looked at Billy—"while I don't wish to seem immodest here, Bill, the investigation, so called, will go where we direct it."

Billy continued to conceal his amusement.

"So?" Marcus said.

"Any drugs moving in the ghetto are yours," I said.

Marcus rolled back in his chair and widened his eyes. He spread his hands.

"Me?" he said.

"And if there is a thorough investigation of the drugs trade in and around Double Deuce, then you are going to be more famous than Oliver North."

"Unless?" Tony said.

"Voilà," I said.

Tony said, "Don't fuck around, Spenser. You want something, say what."

"Move the operation," I said.

"Where?"

"Anywhere but Double Deuce."

"Hawk?" Marcus said.

Hawk nodded.

"Say I could do that? Say I could persuade them to go someplace else?"

"Then you would be as famous as John Marsh."

"Who the fuck is John Marsh?" Tony said.

"My point exactly," I said.

Behind us a train came in, an hour and a half late, from Washington, and people straggled wearily through the bright station.

"Okay," Marcus said.

"Good," I said. "One thing, though."

Marcus waited.

"Kid named Major Johnson," I said. "He's going to have to go down."

"Why?"

"Killed three children," I said.

Marcus shrugged.

"Lots more where he came from," Marcus said.

CHAPTER

37

Susan and I were eating blueberry pancakes and drinking coffee on Sunday morning. The sun was flooding in through the east window of the kitchen, and Susan looked like the Queen of Sheba in a white silk robe, with her black hair loose around her face.

Susan gave Pearl a forkful of pancake.

"Good for her," Susan said. "Whole wheat, fresh fruit, a nice change of pace from bone meal and soy grits."

"Almost anything would be," I said.

"Are you going to put on a shirt," Susan said, "before Jackie arrives?"

"Keep her from flinging herself on me?" I said.

"Sure," Susan said. "Why is she coming over?"

"She didn't say. Just that she needed to talk and would we be home."

Pearl edged her nose under my elbow and pushed my arm.

"Of course," I said.

I cut a wedge from my pancake stack and fed it to her.

"You think we might be spoiling this dog?" I said.

"Of course," Susan said. "But how else will she learn to eat from the table?"

I looked down at Pearl. She was perfectly concentrated on the pancakes, her gaze shifting as one or the other of us ate.

"A canine American princess," I said.

"Nothing wrong with that," Susan said.

The doorbell rang and Susan got up to answer. I left my pancakes and went to the bedroom and put on a shirt. When I came back Pearl was still sitting gazing at my plate, but the plate was empty and clean. I looked at her. She looked back clear eyed and guilt free, alert for another opportunity.

"Ah yes," I said, "a hunting dog."

Susan came back with Jackie. I gave her a half hug and a kiss on the cheek. Pearl jumped around. Susan poured Jackie some coffee. Jackie declined pancakes. I had a few more.

"I'm sorry to intrude on your Sunday morning," Jackie said. "But I have to talk about Hawk."

I nodded.

179

"Puzzling, isn't he," Susan said.

Jackie shook her head.

"You know him," she said to me. "You must know him better than anyone."

I smiled encouragingly.

"I think I'm falling in love with him," Jackie said.

Susan and I both smiled encouragingly.

"But I"—she searched for the right way to say it—"I can't . . . he won't . . ."

"You can't get at him," I said.

"Yes."

Jackie was silent contemplating that, as if having found the right phrase for it, she could rethink it in some useful way.

"I mean, what's not to like? He's fun to be with. He's funny. He knows stuff. He's a dandy lover. . . . But I can't seem to get at him."

I ate some more pancake. I'd made them with buck-wheat flour, and they were very tasty. Jackie was looking at me. I glanced at Susan. This was her area, and I was hoping she'd step in. She didn't, she was looking at me too.

So was Pearl. But all Pearl wanted was food. Dogs are easy.

"Part of what Hawk is," I said, "is that you can't get at him. Erin Macklin thinks that's the price he paid to get out."

"Out of what?" Jackie said. "Being black? Being black's hard on everybody. I don't shut him out."

Susan remained quiet. She looked like someone watching a good movie.

"Well," I said, "if you're a certain kind of guy—"

180

"Guy?" Jackie said. "Guy? Is that it? Some fucking arcane guy shit?"

"Jackie," I said, "I didn't come over to your place and say, 'Let me explain Hawk to you.' "

She took a deep inhale and held it for a moment with her lips clamped together, then she let it out through her nose and nodded.

"Of course you didn't," she said. "I'm sorry. I'm just very stressed."

"Being in love with Hawk would be stressful," I said.

"I don't think I'm in love with him yet. But I will be soon, and I want to figure this out before it's too late."

I nodded. Susan watched.

"You were saying?" Jackie said.

"You have a sense of who you are," I said. "And you're determined to keep on being who you are, and maybe the only way you can keep on being who you are is to go inside, to be inaccessible. Especially, I would think, if you're a black man. And more especially if you do the kind of work Hawk does."

"So why do it?"

"Because he knows how," I said. "It's what he's good at."

"And that means he can't love anybody," Jackie said.

"It means you keep a little of yourself to yourself."

"Why?" Jackie said.

"Suze," I said, "you want to offer any interpretation?"

"No."

I looked at Pearl. She appeared to be fantasizing about buckwheat pancakes.

181

"I don't suppose," I said, "that you'd settle for an elo-quent shrug of the shoulders?"

"Not unless you're willing to admit that you've gotten bogged down in your own bullshit and you don't know how to get out," Jackie said.

"It's not bullshit," I said. "But it is something one feels more than something one thinks about, and it's hard to explain to someone who doesn't live Hawk's life."

"Like a woman?"

I shook my head.

"Hawk sometimes kills people. People sometimes try to kill him. Keeping yourself intact while you do that kind of work requires so much resolution that it has to be carefully protected."

"Even from someone who loves him?"

"Especially," I said.

We were all silent.

"This is probably as much of Hawk as I will ever get," she said.

"Probably," I said.

"I don't think it's enough," Jackie said.

"It might be," Susan said, "if you can adjust your expec-tations."

Jackie looked at Susan and at me.

"You've been lucky," Jackie said. "I guess I'm envious."

Susan looked straight at me and I could feel the connec-tion between us.

"Luck has nothing to do with it," Susan said.

38

Hawk and I were sitting in my office in the late afternoon on a day that made you feel eternal. All the trees on the Common were budded. Early flowers bloomed in the Public Gardens, and the college kids littered the embankment along Storrow Drive, soaking up the rays behind BU.

We'd been asking around after Major for a couple of weeks now. And the more we asked where he was, the more no one knew.

"He'll show up," Hawk said.

"He's maybe killed three people," I said. "Be good if we found him rather than the other way around."

"We'll hear from him," Hawk said. "He's going to have to know."

"Know what you'll do?"

"What I'll do, and what he'll do when I do it," Hawk said.

"You've given him a lot of slack," I said. "I've seen you be quite abrupt with people who were a lot less annoying than Major is."

"Kind of want to see what he'll do too," Hawk said.

"I sort of guessed that you might," I said.

"We'll hear from him," Hawk said.

And we did.

The phone rang just after six, when the sun had pretty well departed, but it was still bright daylight.

"Got a message for Hawk," the voice said. It was Major.

"Sure," I said. "He's here."

I clicked onto speakerphone.

Hawk said, "Go ahead."

"This Hawk?" Major said.

"Un huh."

"You know who this is?"

"Un huh."

"You can't prove I done those people," Major said, "can you?"

"You got something to say, say it."

"Maybe I didn't do them."

"Un huh."

"That all you say?"

Hawk made no response at all.

"You been looking for me," Major said.

"Un huh."

"You can't find me."

"Yet," Hawk said.

"You never find me 'less I want you to."

Again Hawk was silent.

"You find me, you can't do nothing. You got no evidence."

"I know you did it," Hawk said.

"You think I done it."

Hawk was silent.

"So what you do, you find me?"

Hawk didn't say anything.

"What you think you do?"

More silence.

"Can't do shit, man."

"Un huh."

The speaker buzzed softly in the silence. Hawk was leaning his hips against the edge of my desk, arms folded. He looked like he might be waiting for a bus.

"You still there?" Major said.

"Sure."

"Want to meet me?"

"Sure."

"You know the stadium in the Fenway? By Park Drive?" Major said.

"Un huh."

"Be there, five A.M."

"Tomorrow," Hawk said.

185

Again the scratchy silence lingered on the speakerphone, and then Major hung up. I hit the speakerphone button and broke the connection. Hawk looked over at me and grinned.

"Think he's alone?" I said.

"No. They won't leave him."

"Even when Tony Marcus says to?"

"We crate Major and they'll go," Hawk said. "But they won't leave him there."

"And they will probably bother us while we're trying to crate him," I said.

"Only twenty of them," Hawk said.

"Against you and me?" I said. "I like our odds."

Hawk shrugged.

We were quiet for a while, listening to the traffic sound wisp in through the window.

"We don't know he did it," I said.

"You hear him say he didn't?" Hawk said.

"Haven't heard him say he did," I said. "Exactly."

"How you feel 'bout the Easter bunny?" Hawk said.

"Maybe Major's just profiling," I said. "Makes him feel important, being a suspect."

"We see him tomorrow," Hawk said. "We ask him."

39

Hawk was gone and I sat in my office without turning the lights on and looked at the flossy new building across the street. The whole thing at Double Deuce was rolling faster than it should.

Hawk's scenario—and I knew he believed it—made good enough sense. Tallboy had welshed on a drug deal and Major had shot Tallboy's girlfriend and probably by accident the little girl. Then, when Tallboy had felt obliged to revenge it, he wasn't good enough and Major had snuffed him too. Nothing wrong with that. Things like that happened.

I got up and stood looking out the window with my arms folded. So what was bothering me?

One thing was that I figured that tomorrow would escalate, and Hawk would kill Major. Somebody probably would, sooner or later. But I wasn't sure it should be us.

Another thing was that it didn't seem like Major's style. He was a show-off. If Tallboy was holding out, Major would face him off in front of an audience. And he'd brag about it. Just as he'd bragged that Tony Marcus was his supplier. And if there was a murder or two in any deal where Tony Marcus was part of the mix, why wouldn't you wonder about him?

I stood looking out the window and wondered about Tony for a while. It didn't lead me anywhere. Below me on Berkeley Street a man walked three greyhounds on a tripartite leash. There was some sort of organization in town that arranged adoptions for overaged racing dogs. Maybe I should consider a career change.

We would meet Major in the morning. I knew Hawk well enough to know that he wouldn't waver on that. I didn't know him well enough to know why he wouldn't. There was something about Major. There was something going on between them that didn't include me. He'd go whether I went with him or not, and I couldn't let him go alone.

The guy with the greyhounds turned the corner on Stuart Street and headed toward Copley Square. I watched until they disappeared behind the old Hancock Building.

"Well," I said aloud to no one, "better do something."

And since I couldn't think of anything else to do, I got in my car and drove to Double Deuce.

There was a light showing in the window of the second-floor apartment that Hawk and I had rousted. I went up the dark stairs and along the sad corridor toward the light that showed under the partly sprung door. I felt my whiteness more than I had when I'd come with Hawk. Then we'd been chasing something. Now I was an intruder from a land as alien to these kids as Tasmania.

I took a deep breath and let it out slowly and knocked. The sounds of the room stopped and the light went out. I heard a shuffle of footsteps and then a voice said through the closed door:

"Yo?"

The voice had a soft rasp. It was probably Goodyear.

"Spenser," I said. "Alone."

"What you want?"

"Talk."

" 'Bout what?"

"Saving Major's ass," I said.

"He ain't here."

"You'll do," I said. "I don't have a lot of time."

I could hear some whispering, then the door lock slid back and the door opened and I walked into the dark room.

189

CHAPTER

40

When I got home it was nearly 8:30 and the Braves and the Dodgers were on cable. Susan was in the kitchen. There was a bottle of Krug Rosé Champagne in a crystal ice bucket on the counter and two fluted glasses. Susan was wearing a suit the pale green-gold color of spring foliage. It was an odd color, but it went wonderfully with her dark hair. The suit had a very short skirt, too. Pearl was on the couch which occupied most of the far wall in front of the big picture window, where, if you were there at the right time, you could look at the sunset. Now there was only darkness. She cavorted about for a moment to greet me and then went back to her couch.

I looked at the champagne.

"Does this bode well for me?" I said. "Or are you having company?"

"It's to sip while we talk," Susan said. "If you'll open it."

I did and carefully poured two glasses. I gave one to her. She touched its rim to mine and said, "To us."

"I'll drink to that," I said. And we did.

I looked down at her legs, much of which were showing under the short skirt.

"Great wheels," I said.

"Thank you," she said. "I'm afraid I've been a god-damned fool."

"Anything's possible," I said.

We each drank a little more champagne.

"First, to state the obvious, I love you."

"Yes," I said. "I know that."

"Second, and I'm afraid about as obvious, I do better with other people's childhoods than I do with my own."

"Don't we all," I said.

"I was brought up in a well-related suburb by affluent parents. My father went to business, my mother stayed home with the children. My father's consuming passion was business; my mother's was homemaking. I was expected to marry a man who went to business and loved it, to stay home with the children, and make a home."

I didn't say anything. Pearl lay still on the couch, her back legs stretched straight out, her head on her front paws, motionless except for her eyes, which watched us carefully.

191

"And I did," Susan said. She drank another swallow of champagne, and put the glass back on the counter and looked into the glass where the bubbles drifted toward the surface.

"Except that the marriage was awful and there were no children, and I got divorced and had to work and met you."

" 'Bye-'bye, Miss American Pie," I said.

Susan smiled.

"Most of the rest you know," she said. "We both know. When I left Sunnybrook Farm I left with a vengeance—the job, then the Ph.D., moving to the city. Part of your charm at first was that you were so unsuburban. You were dangerous, you were your own and not someone else's. And you gave me room."

I poured some more champagne in her glass, carefully, so it wouldn't foam up and overflow.

"But always I was failing. I wasn't keeping house, I wasn't raising children. I wasn't doing it right. It's one of the reasons I left you."

"For a while," I said.

"And it's the reason I wanted you to live with me."

"Not because I am cuter than a bug's ear?"

"That too," Susan said. "But mostly I wanted to pretend to be what I had never been."

"Which is to say, your mother," I said.

Susan smiled again.

"I'll bet you can claim the thickest neck of any Freudian in the country," she said.

"I'm not sure that's a challenge," I said. "Joyce Brothers is probably second."

192

"And I strong-armed you into moving in, and it hasn't been any fun at all."

"Except maybe last Sunday morning after I let Pearl out," I said.

"Except for that."

We were quiet while we each had some more champagne.

"So what's your plan?" I said.

"I think we should live separately," Susan said. "Don't misunderstand me. I think we should continue to live intimately, and monogamously . . . but not quite so proximate."

"Proximate," I said.

Susan laughed, though only a little.

"Yes," she said, "proximate. I do, after all, have a Ph.D.—from Harvard."

"Nothing to be ashamed of," I said.

"How do you feel about it, living apart again?" Susan said.

"I agree with your analysis and share your conclusion."

"You don't mind?"

"No, I like it."

"It'll be the way it was."

"Maybe better," I said. "You won't be wishing we could live together."

"Where will you go?" Susan said.

"I kept my apartment," I said.

Susan widened her eyes at me.

"Did you really?" she said.

I nodded and drank some more champagne and offered

to pour some more in her glass; she shook her head, still looking at me.

"Not quite a ringing endorsement of the original move," she said.

I couldn't think of an answer to that, so I kept quiet. I have rarely regretted keeping quiet. I promised myself to work on it.

"You knew I was a goddamned fool," she said.

"I knew it was important to you. I trusted you to work it out."

She reached out and patted my hand.

"I did not make a mistake in you," she said.

"No," I said, "you didn't."

The doorbell rang.

Susan said, "I wanted a last supper as roommates."

She smiled a wide genuine smile.

"But I've abandoned pretense. It's the Chinese place in Inman Square that delivers."

I raised my champagne glass.

"À votre santé," I said.

Susan went down and brought up the food in a big white paper sack and put it on top of the refrigerator where Pearl couldn't reach it.

"Before we dine," Susan said, "I thought we might wish to screw our brains out."

"Kind of a salute to freedom," I said.

"Exactly," Susan said.

CHAPTER

41

The Fenway is part of what Frederick Law Olmsted called the emerald necklace when he designed it in the nineteenth century—an uninterrupted stretch of green space following the Charles River and branching off along the Muddy River to Jamaica Pond, and continuing, with modest interference from the city, to Franklin Park and the Arboretum. It was a democratic green space and it remained pleasant through demographic shifts which moved the necklace in and out of bad neighborhoods. Along the Park Drive section of the Fenway the neighborhood was what the urban planners probably called transitional. There were apartments full of nurses and graduate stu-

dents along Park Drive, and across the Fenway there was
the proud rear end of the Museum of Fine Arts. Simmons
College was on a stretch of Fenway, and Northeastern
University was a block away and just up the street was
Harvard Medical School.

But the Fenway itself was a kind of Riviera for both
black and Hispanic gangs taking occasional leave from
their duties in the ghetto. And they didn't have to go far.
The ghetto spread sullenly beyond the Museum and behind the University. The stadium at the southwest end of
the Fenway midsection was dense with gang graffiti.

At two minutes to five in the morning, Hawk and I
parked up on the grass near the Victory Gardens where
Park Drive branches off Boylston Street. We thought it
would be wise to walk in from this end and get a look at
things as we came. There wasn't much traffic yet, and as
we walked into the Fenway the grass was still wet. A hint
of vapor hovered over the Muddy River, and two early
ducks floated pleasantly out from under the arched field-
stone bridge.

"We figured out exactly what we're doing?" I said.

I had on a blue sweatshirt with the sleeves cut off, and
jeans, and white leather New Balance gym shoes. I wore a
Browning 9mm pistol in a brown leather holster tipped a
little forward on my right hip, and a pair of drop-dead Ray
Ban sunglasses.

"Thinking 'bout making a citizen's arrest," Hawk said.
He was wearing Asics Tiger gels, and a black satin-finish
Adidas warm-up suit with red trim. The jacket was half

zipped, and the butt of something that appeared to be an antitank gun showed under his left arm.

"I don't want to kill him if we don't have to," I said.

"He's in the way," Hawk said. "We don't get him out the way we got problems at Double Deuce. Plus he buzzes three people—and he strolls?"

"If he really buzzed three," I said.

"He did, 'less you find me somebody better."

"I'm working on that," I said.

"Better hurry," Hawk said. "Got about thirty-five seconds 'fore the gate opens."

Ahead of us was the stadium, poured concrete with bleacher seats rising up at either end. A skin baseball diamond was at the near end. Another diamond wedged in against the stadium administrative tower at the far end. The place must have been built in the thirties. It had, on a small scale, that neo-Roman look like the LA Coliseum. The tower was closed. It had always been closed. I had never seen it open.

As we came into the open end of the stadium from the north, I could see maybe twenty black kids in Raiders caps sitting in a single line, not talking, in the top row of the bleachers on the east side of the stadium, the sun half risen behind them. We kept coming, and as we did, Major appeared from behind the tower, walking slowly toward us.

Hawk laughed softly.

"Major been watching those Western movies," Hawk said.

Major was all in black. Shirts, jeans, high-topped sneakers, Raiders cap. As he came toward us I could see the sun glint on the surface of a handgun stuck in his belt.

"Piece in his belt," I said. "In front."

"Un huh."

We were in front of the assembled Hobart Raiders now. We stopped. Major, fifteen yards from us, stopped when we stopped. One point for us: you needed to be pretty good to count on shooting well at forty-five feet with a handgun. Hawk and I were pretty good. Odds were that Major wasn't. Odds were on the other hand that if all the kids in the stands opened up, some of them might hit us. Odds were, though, that not all of them had weapons.

"Life's uncertain," I said to Hawk.

Hawk was looking at Major.

"What we need now," Hawk said. "Deep thinking."

"Talked with Goodyear and Shoe last night," I said.

Hawk's eyes moved calmly between Major and the Raiders in the stands.

"They said that Major didn't kill Devona."

"How 'bout Tallboy?" Hawk said.

"Major killed Tallboy because Tallboy came in on them drunk and waving a gun."

"So," Major said, "Hawk, my man, what's happening?"

"Let's see," Hawk said.

"You come to get me? You and the Mickey?"

"Me," Hawk said.

"So why you bring him?"

"Didn't bring him," Hawk said. "He come on his own."

"Make you look like a fucking Tom," Major said.

198

"You invited me, boy," Hawk said. "You got something in mind, whyn't you get to it."

"Good move," I said to Hawk. "Placate him."

Hawk grinned.

"What you smiling for?" Major said. "I don't let no one laugh at me."

Major paused and looked at the gang members in the stands. They were all standing now, motionless along the top row of seats. He was playing to them. He looked back at us.

"You know the fucking law, Hawk. Respect. You like made the fucking law, man. Respect. You don't get treated with respect, you see to it."

"Heard maybe you backshot a fourteen-year-old girl," I said. "Hard not to dis you."

"Fuck you, Irish. I didn't shoot no sly. But if I do, what you know about it? You don't know shit. You live in some kind of big white-ass fucking house, and you drive your fancy white-ass car. And you don't know a fucking thing about me. You live where I live, and what you got is respect, and you ain't got that you ain't got shit. Don't matter who you spike or how, you get respect. Hawk know that. Am I right or wrong, Hawk?"

"Never had to backshoot a fourteen-year-old girl," Hawk said.

"You think I shot her, you think what you fucking want. Everybody know you, Hawk. You the man. You the one set the standard. Well I be the man now, you dig? I set the standard. All of them"—he jerked his head toward the gang members—"they looking at me. I want them here, they here. I let someone dis me, he dis them. That mean some sly got to bite the dust." Major shrugged elaborately. "Plenty of them around," he said. "You know why I the man? I have to do one, I'll do one. There some brothers bigger than me, some Homeboys real strong fighters like John Porter. But he ain't the man, and they ain't the man. I the man. You know why? 'Cause I crazy enough. I crazy enough to do anything. And everybody know. Maybe somebody got to die. I willing. I step up. Ain't afraid to die, ain't afraid at all. I die what I be losing?"

Major paused. Hawk waited.

"So you be thinking I lined Tallboy's wiggle, then you wrong. But if I wanted to I would have and I wouldn't give a fuck what you or the flap or anybody thought 'bout it."

Hawk was perfectly still, and perfectly relaxed like he always was in this kind of moment. But he was different. He didn't, I realized all at once, want to kill Major. I knew he would if he had to, but in all the years I'd known him I'd never seen him want or not want. Killing was a practical matter to Hawk.

"You didn't kill her," Hawk said, "who did?"

"Hawk, you and me the same," Major said. "It got to be done we step up. Ain't afraid to be killing, ain't afraid to be dying."

Major was playing to his audience, and, I realized, he was playing most of all to Hawk.

Quietly I said, "How many guns, you think?"

Hawk said, "Besides Major, probably two or three. Kids

have them, pass them around. Kid with the raincoat probably has a long gun. One with the jacket probably got one."

"What you talking 'bout?" Major said. "You better be
listening to me."

"We arguing which one of us going to fry you," Hawk
said.

"You, Hawk." There was something almost like panic in
Major's voice. "You and me, Hawk. Not me and some
flap-fucking Irish."

I was scanning the crowd in the stands. Hawk was right.
Only two of them wore coats that would conceal a gun.
Some of them might have it stuck under a shirt or in an
ankle holster, but the good odds were to fire at the ones
with coats first.

Major raised his voice. "John Porter."

Around the corner of the grandstand came John Porter
with Jackie Raines. John Porter had her arm and he held a
revolver to her head. Jackie's face was pinched with fear.
She walked stiffly, trying not to be compliant, but not strong
enough to resist John Porter.

"Got this here fine nigger lady," Major said.

Jackie looked at us. Her eyes were wide.

"Hawk," she said. She said it like a request. Hawk didn't
move. His expression didn't change.

"Come around without you," Major said, the laughter
lilting in his voice. "Say we all black folks, and I'm trying
to get the *low-down* on what it's like for you poor nigger
boys in the *ghet-to*. And John Porter he say how come you
don't go *low down* on this?"

201

Major laughed. It was real laughter. It wasn't for effect, but it had a crazy tremolo along its edge. John Porter smiled vacantly, proud to be mentioned by Major.

"So she say I know you gonna meet with Hawk and he won't tell me where. So I say we tell you where, slut. Fact we bring you along with us."

Hawk said to me, "When it starts, you take the stands."

I said, "Um hmm."

Major said, "I tol you, you better be listening to me, Hawk. You want your slut back, you better be paying attention to me."

Hawk looked at Major, full focus, and slowly nodded his head once.

"You want the slut back, you ask me nice, you say please, Mr. Major, and maybe I tell John Porter to let her go."

Hawk's gaze didn't falter. He was waiting. Major didn't know him like I did. Major thought he was hesitant.

"Go ahead, man. Say please, Mr. Major Johnson, sir."

Major was excited. He moved back and forth in a kind of wide-legged strut as he talked. The gun in his belt was a Glock, 9mm, retail price around $550, magazine capacity seventeen rounds. It was enough to make you nostalgic for zip guns.

"Hawk," Jackie said again. "Please."

"Better hurry up, Hawk, better ask me nice and polite, 'fore I put a bullet up her ass."

In the stands a kid in a black satin hip-length warm-up jacket brought an Uzi out from underneath it.

"*No*," Major screamed. "*Nobody shoots!* This is me and Hawk! Nobody shoots! Hawk! Me and Hawk!"

Hawk reached thoughtfully under his arm and brought out the big Magnum. He turned deliberately sideways toward Major and Jackie.

"Hawk," Jackie screamed. "Don't!"

"You shoot at me, Hawk," Major shouted, "John Porter kill the slut." Major's voice was full of high vibrato.

Hawk brought the gun down onto his target.

"Don't!" Jackie screamed again.

"He'll kill her"—Major was screaming now too—" 'less you ask me nice."

I drew my Browning and cocked it as it cleared the holster. Everything seemed to be moving languidly through liquid crystal. Hawk settled the handgun on his target and squeezed off a round and John Porter's face contorted. His gun spun away from him and he flung out both his arms and fell backwards, sprawling on the ground behind Jackie. Jackie was standing with both hands pressed against her open mouth. She looked as if she were trying to scream and couldn't. The kids in the stands were motionless.

Hawk walked slowly toward Major, the big Magnum still in his hand, hanging loosely at his side. When he reached him he looked straight down at Major. And stood, looking at him and not speaking. Then he reached over and took the Glock out of Major's belt and dropped it in his pocket. He looked down at John Porter. John Porter was sitting up now with his left hand pressed against his right shoulder, and some blood slowly showing through his fingers and smearing on the smooth finish of his half-zippered warm-up jacket. There was no pain in his face yet, just surprise, and a kind of numb shock.

"Who iced Devona Jefferson?" Hawk said. He didn't speak very loudly, but his voice seemed too loud in the frightening silence.

I put my gun away and walked over and stood beside Jackie. The first cars of the morning rush hour were beginning to move around the Fenway.

"Who killed her?" Hawk said again.

Major seemed dazed, staring at Hawk as if he'd never seen him before. The ducks had flown, frightened by the gunfire. I put an arm around Jackie's shoulder. No one spoke. No one moved.

Then Major said, "Marcus. Tallboy was skimming on us and Tony say be a good lesson for everybody."

"He didn't do it himself," Hawk said.

"Billy done it," Major said. "Done Tallboy, too, and left him in Double Deuce so we'd see and remember."

"I heard you did Tallboy," I said.

"Tol everybody I did," Major said. "But it was Billy."

"Marcus got to take the jump for it," Hawk said.

Major nodded. He seemed transfixed, gazing at Hawk.

"I want you out of Double Deuce," Hawk said.

Major nodded slowly.

"We gonna go," he said. "Tony already say so."

"Tony going to be gone," Hawk said. "I say so."

Everyone lingered.

Hawk said, "I'll see to John Porter."

"We be going," Major said.

Hawk nodded and Major turned and walked away across the field toward the open end. From the stands the long silent row of black kids in Raider hats went with him, one after the other jumping down off the grandstand and following him in silence.

"He might have killed me," Jackie said.

Hawk was motionless, looking after Major.

"For Christ sake, Hawk," Jackie said. Her voice was still very shaky. "You might have killed me shooting at him."

"No," Hawk said. "I wouldn't have."

Hawk looked down at John Porter for another silent moment. John Porter stared at the ground, waiting for whatever would happen. Then Hawk put the big Magnum back carefully under his arm and looked again at Major, now nearly across the field, with his gang filing after him.

"Can we use him?" I said to Hawk. "Will he stay?"

Hawk nodded. The sun was well up now, and the ducks had returned and were once again paddling in the Muddy River.

"Kid more like me than a lot of people," Hawk said.

CHAPTER

42

Belson and I were sitting at the bar in Grill 23 across the street from police headquarters and two blocks from my office. We were each drinking a martini. I had mine with a twist. Around us were a host of young insurance executives and ad agency creative types wearing expensive clothes and talking frantically about business and exercise. Campari and soda seemed popular.

"One of the Hobart Street Raiders got shot," Belson said.

There were mixed nuts in a cut-glass bowl on the bar. I selected out a few cashews and ate them.

"That so?" I said.

"Dude named John Porter. Somebody dropped him off at City Hospital ER with a slug in his shoulder. John Porter wouldn't say who."

"John Porter?" I said.

"Yeah. You been dealing with the Raiders, haven't you?"

"Small world," I said.

I sipped my drink. It takes awhile acquiring a taste for martinis, but it's worth the effort.

"Raiders have cleared out of the Double Deuce apartments," Belson said. "Packed up and left. Hear from the gang unit that Tony Marcus put out the word."

"Public-spirited," I said.

"Tony? Yeah. Anyway, they're gone."

Belson drank the rest of his martini and ordered another. His were straight-up and made with gin and an olive. Mine was made with Absolut vodka, on the rocks. I ordered one too.

"Just being polite," I said. "Don't want you to feel like a lush."

"Thanks," Belson said. He sorted through the mixed nuts.

"You eating all the cashews?" he said.

"Of course."

"One-way bastard," Belson said.

He found a half cashew and took it, and two Brazil nuts and ate them and sipped from his second martini. His jacket was unbuttoned and I could see the butt of his gun. He wore it in a holster inside his waistband.

207

"Marty and I were talking," Belson said. "Figure who-ever spiked Porter probably did us a favor. Been in and out of jail most of his life. Leg-breaker. Some homicides we could never prove."

We each drank a little. Around us the after-work social scene whirled in a montage of pastel neckties and white pantyhose and perfume and cologne and cocktails, and talk of Stair Masters and group therapy and recent movies.

"Old for a gangbanger," Belson said. "Nearly thirty."

I nodded. I rummaged unsuccessfully for cashews. They were all gone. I ate three hazelnuts instead.

"Kid seemed kind of proud about being shot," Belson said. "Gang kids put a lot of stock in that."

"They got nothing else to put stock in," I said.

"Probably not," Belson said. "But that's not my prob-lem. I investigate shootings. Even if the shooting is maybe necessary, I'm supposed to investigate it."

"And handsomely paid for the work, too," I said.

"Sure."

Belson picked up the martini glass and looked through it along the bar, admiring the refracted colors. Then he took a brief sip and put it down.

"Spenser," Belson said, "Marty and me figure you or Hawk done John Porter. And we probably can't prove it, and if we could, why would we want to?"

"Why indeed," I said.

"But I didn't want you thinking we didn't know."

"I understand that," I said. "And I know that if you thought, say, Joe Broz had done it, that maybe you could prove it, and would."

Belson looked at me silently for a moment, then he drank the rest of his martini in a swallow, put the glass on the bar, and put his right hand out, palm up. I slapped it lightly.

"Tony Marcus killed Devona Jefferson and her baby," I said.

"Himself?"

"He had Billy do it. I got a witness."

I looked around the bar. There were several attractive young executive-class women with assertive blue suits and tight butts. I could ask one to join me for a discussion of Madonna's iconographic impact on mass culture. The very thought made my blood boil.

"Who you got?" Belson said. His drink sat undisturbed in front of him on the bar.

"Major Johnson," I said.

"Kid runs the Hobart Street Raiders."

"Yeah. He was in the truck when she got hit. He won't say so, but he probably ID'd her for Billy."

"And?" Belson said.

"He'll need immunity."

"I can rig that," Belson said. "Can he tie Tony to it?"

"Heard him give the order," I said. "Whole thing supposed to be an object lesson for the gangs. Tony wanted them to remember who was in charge."

Belson nodded.

"Sort of dangerous being the only eyewitness against Tony Marcus," he said.

"We'll protect him," I said.

"You and Hawk?"

"Yeah."

"Still, it's his word against Tony's. Tony ain't much, but neither is the kid."

"Thought of that," I said.

"You got a plan?"

I smiled.

"Surely you jest," I said.

Belson pushed the undrunk martini away from him and leaned his elbows on the bar.

"Tell me," he said.

I did.

CHAPTER

43

International Place nestles in the curve of the High Street off-ramp from the Central Artery, right across the street from the new Rowe's Wharf development on the waterfront. It's about forty stories tall, with a four-story atrium lobby full of marble and glass. In the lobby is a dining space, and at one end of the dining space is a croissant shop. Hawk and I were sitting at one of the little tables in front of the croissant shop, having some coffee and acting just like we belonged there. The glass walls let in the sun and the movement of urban business outside. It was 10:20 in the morning and most of the tables were empty. A roundish young woman at the next table was enjoying

black coffee with artificial sweetener, and a chocolate croissant.

"Tony know the spots, don't he?" Hawk said.

He was wearing a teal silk tweed jacket over a black silk
Tee-shirt, with jeans, and black cowboy boots. He leaned
back in his chair, his legs straight out, his feet crossed
comfortably at the ankles. I had on a blue blazer and sneakers. If there were a *GQ* talent scout in the building, our
careers would be made.

"Major's okay?" I said.

"Yeah. I told him Tony's answer when we said Major
had to take the fall."

" 'Plenty more where he came from'?"

Hawk grinned. "What Major hate was not so much that
Tony would let him take the rap, but that he didn't matter.
Major like to think he important."

"Here's his chance," I said.

We each had a little coffee. We examined some of the
secretaries on coffee break. There was one with sort of
auburn hair whose dress was some kind of spring knit and
fit her very well. We examined her with special care.

"You talked with Jackie?" I said.

"Un huh."

"How was that?"

"Jackie don't like shooting," Hawk said.

"Nothing wrong with that," I said.

"Except that I'm a shooter," Hawk said.

The woman with the auburn hair and the knit dress got
up and walked out of the dining area. We watched her go.

"She said she couldn't love no shooter," Hawk said.

I nodded.

"I said did she want me to get a paper route?"

"Nice compromise," I said.

Hawk grinned.

"Jackie said that maybe there was a third alternative. She talks like that, *third alternative*. I said I was a little long in the tooth for *third alternatives*."

"Never too late," I said.

Hawk was silent for a moment. His face showed nothing, but his gaze was very heavy on me.

"Yeah, it is," Hawk said. "Too late for me to be something else a long time ago. Anything but what I am is a step down."

"Yes," I said.

"You're smart," Hawk said. "You could do other things."

I shrugged.

"How come you do this?" Hawk said.

"It's what I know how to do," I said. "I'm good at it."

Hawk grinned.

"You want to be good at selling vinyl siding?"

"Rather die," I said.

"Jackie don't quite get that," Hawk said.

A new coffee break shift appeared. Hawk and I were alert to it, but no one compared to the one with the auburn hair.

"Tony's late," Hawk said.

"Surprising," I said, "seeing as there's some kind of sweet glop to be eaten."

213

A blonde woman in pale gray slacks went up and got a cappuccino and a whole-wheat roll and came back past us. She was wearing a nice perfume.

"So Jackie's gone?" I said.

"Un huh."

"Too bad," I said.

Hawk shrugged.

"You care?" I said.

"Don't plan to," Hawk said.

"She was a nice woman," I said.

"Un huh."

"You love her?" I said.

"You really bored?" Hawk said, "or what."

"No, I just figured Susan would ask me, and if I said I hadn't asked she would have shaken her head without saying anything. Now, if she does it, she'll be implying something about you, not me."

Hawk grinned again.

"You believe in love," he said.

"I have reason to."

"Yeah, maybe," Hawk said. "But you have reason to because you believe in it, not the other way around."

"How'd we end up," I said, "talking about me?"

Hawk made a self-deprecating gesture with his hands as if to say, *It was easy.*

"It never seemed a good idea to believe in it," Hawk said. "Always seemed easier to me to stay intact if you didn't."

We were quiet. The coffee was gone. The sun that had

slanted in and squared our table had moved on toward the service bar.

"Erin was right," I said.

"About me?" Hawk said.

"Yeah," I said. "You've paid a big price."

"Never said I didn't."

"And sometimes it hurts," I said.

It was as far as I'd ever pushed him.

"Un huh."

It was as far as he'd ever gone.

CHAPTER

44

Across the dining area, Tony Marcus came strolling in from the outer lobby. Billy loomed behind him. Tony saw us across the room and they came to the table.

"Get me couple of those chocolate croissant," Marcus said. "Some coffee, three sugars, lotta cream."

Billy went silently to the counter. I'd never heard him speak. Would he order or just point at what he wanted? Marcus sat. He spoke to Hawk. He always spoke to Hawk. Unless he had to, he never spoke to me, or looked at me.

"What do you need now, Hawk?" Tony said.

"Need somebody to take the fall for Devona and Crystal Jefferson," Hawk said. "Told you that before."

216

"And I gave you the kid, Johnson," Marcus said.

"He didn't do it," Hawk said.

Marcus shrugged. "So what? He probably did something. Bag him for this."

"You did it, Tony."

Marcus shrugged again. "So what?"

"You wanted to remind the gang kids how tough you were. Must be a little tricky doing business with the gang kids, them being kind of crazy and all."

"You got that right," Marcus said.

"So you had Billy ace the kid, Devona."

"Got their attention," Marcus said. "Nobody saw the baby." Another shrug. "Shit happens."

Billy came back with the coffee and croissants, and Marcus bit off half of one and chewed it carefully.

"Billy used a nine," Hawk said.

Billy was standing near his boss, blocking out most of the light on that side of the room. Hawk leaned back a little more in his chair and looked at him.

"I'll bet you didn't get rid of it," Hawk said. "Dump some fourteen-year-old ghetto broad—who's going to notice? I'll bet you still got the piece."

Billy made an almost indiscernible gesture toward his right hip and caught himself. Hawk grinned.

"Bet you carrying it now," Hawk said.

Marcus finished chewing his croissant.

He said, "Cut the bullshit, Hawk. So Billy dusted the kid, so I told him, so the kid thinks he'll testify. So what? That's all bullshit. Even if he gets to talk, nobody is going to

217

believe him, a gangbanger punk? I got twenty people will swear Billy and I were playing cards in Albany, Georgia, when it happened."

"Albany, Georgia?" I said.

"Wherever you like," Marcus said. "So cut the bullshit and tell me what you want."

Hawk grinned at him. Across the room, Quirk and Belson strolled in from the outer lobby and walked toward the table. Marcus didn't notice. There were a couple of other cops that I recognized, in plainclothes, lingering near the entryway. Hawk opened his teal jacket and there was a microphone pinned to the black silk Tee-shirt.

"Peekaboo," Hawk said.

Marcus stared at the microphone.

"A wire," he said. "You wore a fucking wire on me, you Tom motherfucker."

"Told you somebody had to roll over for those two girls," Hawk said.

Quirk and Belson arrived at the table.

"Say all the legal shit to them, Frank," Quirk said. "Billy—give me the piece you're carrying."

Belson began to recite the formalized litany of arrest like a kid reciting the alphabet. Billy looked at Marcus. Marcus wasn't looking at him. He was still staring at Hawk.

"*Now, Billy.*" Quirk's voice had an edge to it.

Billy lunged past him. Quirk seemed to barely notice, as if he were thinking of something else. But he made some sort of efficient compact movement and Billy hit the floor like a foundered walrus. Quirk held Billy's right arm at an awkward angle with his left hand and reached around and took the Browning off Billy's hip. It was stainless, with a walnut handle.

"Nice piece. Don't you have one like it?"

Without pausing in his recitation, Belson produced a clear plastic bag and held it open and Quirk dropped the gun into it.

"Mine's only got the black finish," I said, "and a black plastic handle. Got a nice white dot on the front sight, though."

Belson finished his recitation and they cuffed Tony Marcus and Billy and hauled them off. Marcus kept staring at Hawk until he was out of sight.

"I think he feels betrayed," I said.

Hawk nodded, looking around the room. Everyone there was staring at us or trying not to.

"You think that the red hair and tight dress will come back in here for lunch?" he said.

45

Susan and I were having supper on Rowe's Wharf, across from International Place in the dining room at the Boston Harbor Hotel. I had an Absolut martini on the rocks, with a twist. Susan had a glass of Riesling, which she probably wouldn't finish.

"Was it the gun?" Susan said.

"Yes," I said.

"Can they convict him with it?" Susan said.

"The gun, the tape, Major's testimony. Sure."

"I'm surprised that Major is willing to testify."

"Hawk says he will."

"Because Hawk told him to?" Susan said.

"Yeah, I imagine so. And, too, it's a chance to be important."

"Interesting, isn't it. He had to know that Hawk could beat him."

"Established the command structure," I said. "I guess any order is better than none."

Susan rested her chin on her upturned palm. The twilight glancing in off the harbor highlighted her huge dark eyes.

"I talked with Jackie," Susan said.

"Too much for her?" I said.

"Yes," Susan said. "She's—overwhelmed, I guess, is the best way to describe it."

"Not just the violence," I said.

"No," Susan said. "She saw Hawk, I suppose, for the first time."

"He saved her life," I said.

"She knows that," Susan said. "But there might have been another way. He shot right past her head to do it without a moment's hesitation."

"It was the best way," I said.

Susan nodded. "Yes, I'm sure it was. Maybe even Jackie is sure it was, but she can't . . . do you see? She can't be with a man who could do that."

"I see," I said. "Could you?"

"I am," Susan said.

I drank some of my martini. I checked the glass. There were at least two swallows left.

"You think we'll see her again?" I said.

With her chin still in her hand, Susan shook her head slowly. The waiter brought menus. We read them. The waiter came back. We ordered. The waiter left. The twilight softened into darkness outside the window, and the harbor water, wavering against the wharf, was very black.

"What do you think?" Susan said. "Is there a future for Major and those other kids?"

"I doubt it," I said.

The waiter returned with food. I mastered the desire for maybe thirteen more martinis, and when Susan and I finished supper and left, I was still sober. It made me proud. We drove back to Cambridge and I parked in the driveway of her place on Linnaean Street.

"You don't think any of them will make it?" Susan said.

"Kids in Double Deuce?" I said. "No, probably not."

"Hawk did," Susan said.

"Sort of," I said.

"That's an awfully grim view," she said.

I shrugged.

"Maybe I'm wrong," I said.

She leaned her head back against the seat cushion.

"Well, as you always say, 'It's never over till it's over.' "

"Yes," I said.

I could see insects little bigger than dust motes swarming in the streetlight, an occasional moth among them.

"First night apart," she said.

"Yeah."

She put her hand out and I took it and we were quiet for a while. Then she spoke.

"I have to say something."

"Sure," I said.

"I'm looking forward to being alone."

"Me too," I said.

"God, what a relief."

"I know," I said.

"See you this weekend," she said.

"Yes," I said. "I'll pick Pearl up tomorrow night for a sleepover. Like before."

"Yes."

Susan leaned toward me in the dark and gave me a long, happy kiss.

"I love you," she said and got out of the car. I watched her until she was inside, then pulled out and drove back across the river to my place on Marlborough Street.

The apartment was stuffy and I walked through it opening windows so that the spring night could circulate. Then I went into the kitchen and took some vodka from the freezer and some vermouth from under the sink and made a large martini over ice with a twist. I put it on the bedside table to let the ice work while I showered and toweled off, and turned back the bed, and got in. I propped up the pillows and turned on the television with the remote. The Braves were still in first place, and they were playing the Giants on cable. Fifth inning, Ron Gant hitting. I sipped my martini and watched the ball game and listened to Skip Caray.

Alone.

I could feel myself smiling. Gant spiked a double into the left-field corner. I took another sip and spoke aloud in the dark room.

"Perfect," I said.